DREAMLAND

By Tom Gilling

The Sooterkin
Miles McGinty
Dreamland

DREAMLAND
TOM GILLING

headline
review

First published in Great Britain in 2008 by
HEADLINE REVIEW
An imprint of HEADLINE PUBLISHING GROUP

1

Cataloguing in Publication Data is available from the British Library

ISBN 978 0 7553 0213 0

Typeset in GarmdITC Bk BT by Palimpsest Book Production Ltd,
Grangemouth, Stirlingshire

Printed and bound in Great Britain by
Clays Ltd, St Ives plc

Headline's policy is to use papers that are natural, renewable and
recyclable products and made from wood grown in sustainable forests.
The logging and manufacturing processes are expected to conform to
the environmental regulations of the country of origin.

For Ciaran

I

The Crypt nightclub on Oxford Street was a crimson cube of blistered concrete and weeping gutters, diagonally across the road from the Supreme Court. Its metal awning hung like a half-closed eyelid above the pavement, where at 10.59 p.m. on New Year's Eve a queue of emaciated clubbers was already forming in the sheep race between the barriers and the wall.

Nick Carmody joined the end of the queue. He'd spent the last couple of hours perched on a window stool in the Judgment Bar, watching a human statue startle passers-by. Painted gold and standing on a milk crate, the statue would suddenly reach out and prod pedestrians with his trident. You expected a kind of serenity from a human statue but this one was so aggressive that Nick kept waiting for someone to turn around and pull him off his pedestal. The fact that he was still standing as the clock approached midnight owed less to the tolerance of New Year's revellers, Nick suspected, than to the presence of two paddy wagons on Taylor Square.

The Crypt wasn't Nick's sort of place. It never had been his sort of place, though he'd been there on the night it opened, drinking bottles of Steinlager as a personal guest of the proprietor, his old classmate Danny Grogan. Danny had been a resentful boarder at St Dominic's since the age of seven, although the Grogan family home, with its bluestone turrets and flagpole, was visible from the school playing fields.

Nick was a scholarship boy from Maroubra Beach. A wary friendship developed between them; an alliance of outsiders.

Since leaving St Dominic's he and Danny had made the effort to meet up from time to time, although there was now a sense – at least to Nick – that what lay behind these encounters was something other than friendship, or even the memory of it.

The queue behind him now stretched around the corner. Nick gazed along the line of faces, searching for a girl – any girl – he would not feel absurd trying to chat up. He was twenty-nine and none of them looked older than – fifteen?

The phone message from Danny had described it as a wake. Of course, this being the Crypt, there was a dress code, which Nick had ignored. The dead boy (even now, Nick found it impossible to think of him as an adult) was their contemporary at St Dominic's, Julian Glazer. He'd just been found at the bottom of a cliff near Bondi Beach, steeped in Jim Beam, with a head wound that could have been the result of falling but could equally have been made to look that way. Nick hadn't seen Glazer since the day they left school, but Danny had made it sound as though he ought to be there – as though he had something to gain by coming.

It wasn't as if he had anywhere else to go. He wondered what Carolyn was doing, then realised he didn't need to wonder. Carolyn would be at a New Year's Eve party, probably at the harbourside home of one of her legal colleagues. They – the few who didn't know – would be asking where Nick was and she'd tell them, as she'd been telling everyone, that she and Nick had called it a day. *Called it a day* – the sort of phrase her father was always using. Carolyn's parents fought like cat and dog but it would never have occurred to either of them to call it a day. Whereas their daughter had called it a day after just seven years. Not that they were married or had children, thank God. Nick would have been tempted to give it a bit longer but in the end he'd had to agree that seven years was long enough. He was surprised – horrified, in a way – to find how little he missed Carolyn, how quickly he'd adjusted to the absence of the woman he'd once imagined spending the rest of his life with. He'd anticipated a difficult few months of mutual hostility and recrimination but what he'd felt instead was relief. Sadness, too, but mostly just relief.

There were two bouncers. From what Nick could see they were turning away as many people as they were letting in. The pair of girls in front of him were clutching cards: tickets to the wake of someone they'd probably never heard of. Typically, Danny hadn't bothered with a formal invitation, just a terse message on Nick's voicemail.

The girls were standing with their arms in the air being frisked. For what, Nick wondered. Pills? Cameras? Weapons? Or was being groped by the bouncers just part of the cover charge?

He half-recognised one of them, or thought he did. Somewhere beneath her Gothic disguise she resembled the daughter of one of his colleagues at the *Daily Star* – a gamine teenager who used to sit in the staff canteen on Sunday afternoons with her Nintendo while her father hammered away upstairs at his weekend football round-up. Even if it was her, she and Nick had only exchanged a few dozen words five years ago, and this was hardly the moment to jog her memory. He half smiled and got a half-scowl in return and decided it probably wasn't her after all.

5

The bigger of the two bouncers had his palm on Nick's chest. 'Ticket?'

'My name's on the door,' said Nick.

'Yeah?' answered the bouncer, looking down the list on the clipboard dangling from his neck. 'And what name is that?'

'Carmody. Nick Carmody.'

The man didn't look like the steroid-crafted automatons Nick was used to meeting outside Sydney's nightclubs. With his gelled hair, olive skin, white shirt and cufflinks he looked more like a guest at an Italian wedding. He let go of the clipboard. 'Sorry, mate,' he said. 'Name's not on the list.'

You're not sorry and we're not mates, Nick wanted to say. 'Look,' he replied. 'Danny Grogan asked me to be here.'

'Show me the invitation.'

'We spoke on the telephone.'

'Listen, mate. If your name's not on the list, you're not coming in. It's as simple as that. No invitation, no entry. This is a private party.'

'It's a wake, not a party,' said Nick. 'And Mr Grogan invited me personally.'

The small group behind Nick – each of them holding a ticket – was becoming impatient. Nick wasn't sure why he was even arguing. The bouncer was refusing him entry to a club he had no desire to enter in the first place. He was only here because Danny had invited him. Nick pushed his right hand into his pocket. The bouncer watched, vaguely curious as to what he might do next. Nick's wallet was full of business cards, souvenirs of his protean reporting career at the *Daily Star*. Most of his colleagues disposed of their old business cards the moment a new set arrived from the printers but Nick always kept a few in his wallet: a portfolio of his former selves. There was a journalists' code of ethics that, among other things, prohibited misrepresentation, but three years of consorting with criminals and corrupt police had taught Nick to interpret the code loosely. He wasn't above flashing an old business card when the need arose, as it did from time to time. His fingers hovered for a moment over a card that said:

NICK CARMODY

ENTERTAINMENT REPORTER

He was on the verge of pulling out the card when he noticed a familiar hawkish profile standing on the corner. He called out, 'Bruce.'

The hawkish profile turned slightly. For the great self-publicist he was, Bruce Myer had always seemed self-conscious about hearing his name. Myer spat the boiled lolly, or whatever it was he was sucking, into a paper tissue which he then disposed of in the pocket of his peach-coloured suit. Nick walked towards him. 'Bruce. Am I glad to see you.' He extended his right hand. 'Nick. Nick Carmody. The *Daily Star.* You fixed me up for the Elton concert.'

'Of course I did . . . Nick . . . how nice to see you.' Myer paused. 'I think we got a few words out of you, didn't we?'

Elton had been in his cocaine and powdered wig phase; Nick had panned the concert without mercy. 'It was a great night,' he said.

'They were all great nights,' Myer remarked ruefully.

Now in his sixties, Myer liked to think of himself as the doyen of Sydney publicists. When the Crypt had first opened its doors Danny Grogan used to fly in the odd big-name British or American DJ to work the turntables for a night and Bruce Myer often handled the publicity, though his own tastes ran more to Bruckner and Judy Garland.

It was said that Myer would advertise his own funeral if he could be sure of getting a couple of paragraphs in the next day's *Herald*. It was probably Myer himself who'd said it, back in the days when his name was on every second hoarding in Sydney, before he let his own publicity go to his head and tried his luck as a promoter. As a publicist you couldn't lose money – Sydney was a publicist's town – but as a promoter you couldn't help it, and Bruce Myer Promotions went bankrupt inside two years.

'Don't tell me you're behind this,' said Nick.

Myer looked aghast. 'No, no . . . Julian's parents asked me to represent them. You'd know how awkward these things can be. I'm just – how shall I put it – managing the message. If you know what I mean.'

Nick knew exactly what Myer meant. Marks Park, where Glazer had been wandering before he stepped off the cliff, was a notorious gay beat. Somehow Myer had managed to keep the precise location out of the papers. Nick only knew about it after speaking to an old mate in the police.

Myer looked around distractedly. 'Did you know him?'

'We were at school together.'

'Poor fellow.'

Nick nodded. The Glazer he remembered was a fat timid boy whose father owned a string of laundromats. Nick remembered hearing jokes about front loaders and rear loaders – trivial schoolboy stuff, but Glazer probably hadn't seen it that way. He'd never thought of Glazer as being a friend of Danny's – but then what did he really know about Danny these days? Apart from what he read in the paper, and occasionally what he wrote in the paper, not much. If Glazer was a friend of Danny's, good luck to him. And if not . . . what did it matter anyway? The poor bastard was dead.

'So what have they got you doing now, Mick?'

'Nick,' said Nick.

'I beg your pardon. Nick.'

Since his brief incarnation as the *Star*'s second-string rock critic, Nick had done the standard Cook's tour of reporting jobs (property, courts, local government) before winding up as the paper's crime reporter, with his own tiny office beside the stationery cupboard. But for a two-bit villain named Darren Milhench, Nick would still have been the *Star*'s crime reporter. While out on parole, Milhench had broken his pregnant fiancée out of the remand section at Mulawa Correctional Centre. The pair fled west and for the next few weeks Milhench had taunted the authorities with phone calls to the media, earning himself a catchy sobriquet: the Phonecard Bandit. A caravan park attendant on the south coast recognised the fiancée and Nick had received the tip-off ahead of the police. Nick had always intended to share his information, but not until he had his exclusive. The fact that Milhench and his fiancée absconded before the tactical operations group arrived wasn't his fault – the police had gone to the wrong caravan park – but Nick found himself the scapegoat, accused by a hysterical police minister of conspiracy to obstruct justice. Since then Nick had been cooling his heels on the *Star*'s foreign subeditors' desk.

'This and that,' he replied.

'Wait a minute.' A lopsided grin spread across the publicist's face. 'Carmody. Nick Carmody . . . the Phonecard Bandit. You're the one who found him.'

Nick shrugged.

'He had the cheek to ask me to represent him.'

'Milhench?'

'The fiancée, actually. She was rather a charming girl. Told me her boyfriend was writing a book and needed an agent. I reminded her that I'd handled Patrick White's first play. I don't think she knew who I was talking about. Anyway, I told her I'd love to represent her boyfriend only my books were full.'

'Listen, Bruce,' said Nick. 'Do you think you could get me in? My name was supposed to be on the door but—'

'But someone left it off by mistake. It happens all the time, Nick. Of course I'll get you in.'

Until Danny Grogan got hold of it, the Crypt had been the Church of St Sophia, a dilapidated shell that provided solace to the second-hand building trade through looted supplies of lead flashing and copper pipe. Danny had saved it from demolition with a couple of million dollars from the family trust fund and turned it into one of Sydney's hippest venues.

The main room was long and low and narrow. Rusty dance cages stretched from floor to ceiling. The décor – or what Nick could see of it in the crepuscular strobe lighting – evoked an S&M dungeon, mock-stone walls adorned with whips and chains and leather masks. The whole room pulsed with sound: 'Temptation', by New Order – one of Nick's favourite songs, and incidentally one of Carolyn's too. (Which was ironic, Nick couldn't help thinking, since of all the people he knew, none was less susceptible to temptation than Carolyn.) The Crypt was a goldmine, as notorious for its stratospheric bar prices and strategic lack of air-conditioning as for its regular drug raids and fire safety violations.

Nick looked about for Danny, or at least for the still point in the crowd that might imply his presence.

As the only son of Harry Grogan, billionaire founder and chairman-for-life of Grogan Constructions, Danny would have been a celebrity even without the Crypt.

From its beginnings as a subcontractor in the outer western suburbs of Sydney, Grogan Constructions had turned itself into one of the powerhouses of the Australian building industry – the developer, manager and majority owner of the Dreamland hotel on the north shore of Sydney Harbour. A Byzantine network of family trusts owned more than half the company and controlled nearly 75 percent of the voting stock. Analysts attributed the lion's share of its billion-dollar valuation to faith in Harry Grogan himself, whose genius in staring down his creditors and pulling the company back from the brink of bankruptcy was the stuff of stock market legend.

The Crypt was a symbol of Danny's rejection of the future his father had planned for him, the rejection of his inheritance. By the age of twenty-nine, playboy Danny was supposed to have metamorphosed, under the inspirational example of his father and the shadowy cabal of American executives who ran the company, into hard-headed Daniel, heir apparent and future CEO of Grogan Constructions. Danny was the dynasty in waiting, and he didn't want any part of it. Meanwhile the Crypt had made him a rich man – and a staple of the tabloids and weekly magazines.

A year ago Danny had got himself on the cover of *Who*

Weekly, dancing with Dannii Minogue. Nick remembered the cheesy cover line: DANNY HITS THE CRYPT WITH DANNII. There were hints in the article that they were – or were about to become – an item, although Dannii's people soon scotched that. Danny had spoken to Nick just as the next week's issue (DANNY AND DANNII – IT'S OVER) hit the news-stands. It had been a fiction from the start but Danny played it for all it was worth. He was coolly disparaging of his media image but at the same time in thrall to it: as if some part of him actually believed the rubbish that was written about him. And at some level, of course, the rubbish was true. The more they wrote about Danny's glamour and notoriety, the more glamorous and notorious he became.

At the bar Nick discovered that he didn't have enough for a bottle of Steinlager and had to settle for tomato juice. Glancing at the angled mirror above the bar, he finally caught sight of Danny. He had his arm around a wasted-looking girl – she couldn't have been more than seventeen – who was trying to drag him away.

Nick called out his name.

Danny turned around. He was high on something, Nick realised. Danny stared at him for a few seconds. He seemed to have trouble focusing and Nick wasn't sure Danny recognised him. Finally he murmured, 'Nick.'

'Thanks for putting my name on the door.'

Danny nodded vaguely.

'I was being sarcastic,' said Nick. 'Your bouncer wouldn't let me in.'

Danny kept staring, and shifting his focus. Behind him, Nick recognised a couple of faces from St Dominic's. He couldn't

12

put a name to either of them but he thought he remembered the taller man as one of Glazer's chief tormentors. St Dominic's didn't have the kudos or the sporting heritage of most of its rivals but made up for it by charging the highest fees. The school had been named after St Dominic (1170–1221), founder of the Dominican order and patron saint of astronomers, but a more plausible guardian, Nick had come to realise, was his namesake St Dominic Savio (1842–1857), patron saint of juvenile delinquents. There was something about the dynamics of power and wealth at St Dominic's that Nick had never been able to understand because he was excluded from it. It wasn't the immorality of privilege; it was the amorality of privilege – a sense of entitlement that belonged, in some macabre way, to both Glazer and his schoolboy persecutors. This wake was the perfect expression of that amorality – a send-off for a dead man that nobody could remember liking, in a converted church where the bouncers sold drugs to under-age dancers.

The girl was still trying to pull Danny away. She shot a fierce glance at Nick and said, 'Danny's sick.'

He didn't look sick to Nick. He looked frightened and disoriented. 'Danny,' said Nick. 'Are you all right?'

'He's fine,' the girl insisted.

'You just told me he was sick.'

'He is sick. I'm taking him home – aren't I, Danny?'

Danny didn't answer.

Nick put a hand on his shoulder. 'There was something you wanted to tell me.' He didn't know whether that was true or not. Information came to Danny: because of who he was, because of who his father was. Sometimes he gave Nick a story to see what he would do with it. Maybe that was why

Danny had invited him here. Maybe it was why Nick had come. But Danny could hardly speak.

'You should get him home,' said Nick.

'Yeah,' the girl said. 'That's where we're going, isn't it, Danny?'

She kept looking for his consent although it seemed to Nick that in the state Danny was in, he would have consented to anything.

'Call me,' said Nick, although even as he said it he knew Danny wasn't going to.

A taxi pulled up outside the club and disgorged three girls onto the pavement. Nick thought about getting in, then changed his mind. A walk would do him good.

He wandered past the cafes and pubs and pizza shops and turned left into Crown Street. In a cobbled lane near the primary school, a metallic blue Audi TT coupe sat among the overflowing wheelie bins – not so much parked as abandoned. A sign beside it said 'No Standing'. Even without its customised numberplate, CR1PT, Nick would have recognised the car as Danny Grogan's.

The Audi's offside headlight was broken and the wing panel and passenger door were dented. The engine was still warm. Nick looked through the passenger window. A small sequined handbag was lying on the seat. The glove box door gaped open, but the glove box was empty.

It was a ten-minute walk from here to the Crypt. Yet Danny had his own private parking spot at the back of the club. Why would he have got out and walked, Nick wondered. He stared at the handbag on the passenger seat. Either Danny hadn't trusted himself to drive – or someone else hadn't.

Nick crossed the road and lit a cigarette and kept walking. He thought about what had happened at the club. He'd turned up because Danny had implied there might be something in it for him – but what? Danny was always good for a tip-off, a piece of second-hand underworld gossip worth a few paragraphs on page three of the *Star*. But in the back of Nick's mind there lurked a hope of something bigger: the story, the real story behind the fire that claimed three lives and made Harry Grogan a millionaire. If Nick was honest about it, that was the reason he couldn't let go of Danny. So tonight wasn't going to be the night. There would be other nights, other letdowns. It was a story worth waiting for.

A nearly full moon hung over the city skyline. Nick was conscious of being followed – not by a person but by a dog. The dog was sitting – or rather, crouching – on the pavement, about twenty metres behind him. Nick had noticed it sitting forlornly under a tree in Prince Alfred Park. It looked like a greyhound. That is, it had the shape of a greyhound but not, somehow, the elastic quiver that a greyhound ought to have. They had locked eyes and the animal had taken this brief intimacy as an invitation to accompany Nick to wherever he might be going. Nick faced the dog and tried to shoo it away but the greyhound just cocked its head and stayed where it was. Nick glanced at his watch. It was after midnight. He turned the corner into Abercrombie Street and kept on walking.

For six weeks – ever since he'd come home to find Carolyn typing her reasons for splitting up on his laptop – Nick had been sleeping in the spare bedroom of a crumbling Victorian terrace in Abercrombie Street, Chippendale. The house belonged to a fellow subeditor at the *Star*, Sally Grabowsky. Sally was divorced and had a three-year-old, Jessica, who liked Nick but was confused as to his status in the household, referring to him usually as 'Nick' but sometimes, disconcertingly, as 'Daddy'. Her real daddy, according to the solicitor's last reported sighting, was working on a prawn trawler somewhere in the Gulf of Carpentaria.

Nick lay in bed, half listening to the ritual early-morning negotiation between mother and daughter over what Jess could have for breakfast if she promised to feed herself. Children had never actually been a subject of conversation with Carolyn, though Nick suspected he had the makings of a good father. Sharing a house with Jess had reinforced this impression. It surprised him how much he could enjoy talking nonsense with someone else's three-year-old.

He thought about Danny Grogan's car and wondered whether it was still where Danny had left it. Chances were it had been towed away and was sitting in a pound somewhere. According to a gossip column Nick remembered reading, in three years Danny Grogan had racked up more than half the cost of his Audi TT in parking fines.

It was 6.55 a.m. on the first day of the new year and the sky behind the cheap venetian blind was overcast, although the temperature was already climbing.

Nick rolled onto his chest and pulled a pillow over his head. The extortionate price of drinks at the Crypt had saved him from the hangover he probably deserved. He lay for a while, trying to go back to sleep, until he heard Jess calling his name. He dragged the pillow off his head. Sally was telling Jess not to wake him, but Jess was taking no notice. She was standing directly outside his door, ordering him to get out of bed.

He got up and pulled on a pair of shorts and walked across the worm-eaten cypress floorboards. He opened the door and looked down. His mouth felt dry and metallic. 'Jess,' he grunted. 'What can I do for you?'

She reached for his hand and tugged him towards the stairs. 'There's a dog outside. It won't go away.'

Nick shrugged.

'Mummy says it's been sitting there all night. She heard it crying.' Jess frowned.

'Dogs don't cry, Jess,' Nick said reassuringly, although he knew it wasn't true. Dogs cried, just as men cried.

'Mummy says we've got to ring the dog catcher and he'll come and take it away.'

'That sounds like a sensible idea.'

'I don't want the dog catcher to take it away.'

Sally was standing in the hallway, studying the dog through the security grille. It was the greyhound that had followed Nick down Cleveland Street in the early hours of the morning.

'I can't see a collar,' said Sally. 'I suppose that means it's been abandoned by its owner.'

The difference between dog-lovers and dog-tolerators, Nick knew, was in the pronoun: dog tolerators, like his father, habit-ually referred to them as 'it', whereas dog-lovers, like his mother, always gave them a gender. Jess was instinctively a dog-lover but, at three, was under the grammatical spell of her dog-tolerating mother.

Gingerly, Nick descended the stairs. 'Come on, Jess. Let's have a look at him.'

'Don't you go near it, Jess,' said Sally. 'It might bite you.'

'I don't think he's a biter,' said Nick. The dog's ears were down; it looked more anxious than aggressive.

'How can you be sure?'

'I've seen this dog before. Last night. In the park.'

'You mean you brought it home?'

'God, no. I thought I'd got rid of him.' Nick squatted down beside the animal. 'He must have followed me.'

'It's a greyhound, isn't it?'

'An arthritic greyhound,' said Nick, patting the animal's sleek skull. 'But I'd say it's been a few years since he's chased any rabbits.'

'I'll ring the pound,' said Sally. Then, 'I can't. It's New Year's Day.'

'Let's give it some milk,' said Jess.

Nick laughed. 'Dogs don't really drink milk, Jess. But I'm sure he'd like some water.'

The greyhound watched Nick, as though sensing its fate lay in his hands.

'It wants to come inside,' said Jess.

Sally glanced at Nick, then at the dog. 'Take it through to the backyard. I suppose it can stay there till we've decided what to do with it.'

Nick trotted the greyhound down the hallway and through the kitchen and out into the vine-smothered concrete rectangle described by the agent who'd sold Sally the house as an 'inner-city entertainer's paradise'. Then he took a cereal bowl from the sink and filled it with water and placed the bowl between the dog's front paws. While Jess stood sentry at the back door Sally asked, 'How was the wake?'

Nick thought for a few moments before answering. 'Weird,' he said at last. 'Something about it reminded me of the Borgias.'

'Sounds interesting. I wish I'd been invited.'

In the two months he'd been sleeping, as a friend/tenant, in Sally's spare bedroom, Nick had become accustomed to these casual inquisitions. He wasn't sure what they meant, or if they meant anything at all. He had known Sally since before she and Randy had started going out. Somewhere in the dim and distant past Nick could picture Randy, in black leather trousers, waiting for her at midnight outside the *Star* with a cigarette in his mouth and two motorcycle helmets under his arm. He'd observed, from one side only, the fireworks of their separation. It was obvious to Nick that, whatever Randy had or hadn't done, deep down Sally still hoped they could get back together again. Sally was clever and funny and attractive. Nick had fancied her from the first time he'd laid eyes on her. But he didn't want to be the one to prove to her that she was still in love with Randy.

'It was for that friend of yours who committed suicide, wasn't it?'

Nick patted his pockets for cigarettes. Sally didn't like him smoking in front of Jess but it made him feel better to know where they were, to know he could light one if he had to.

'He fell off a cliff,' he said. 'I'm not sure it was suicide.'

'Oh.' She waited for him to elaborate. When he didn't she asked, 'What was it then?'

Nick shrugged. He remembered the look on the faces of the two he'd recognised from St Dominic's – as if they knew they were untouchable. 'My guess is it will be an open finding.'

'I wasn't asking you about the finding.'

They stared at each other for a while.

'You should have stayed in with us and watched the fireworks on TV,' said Sally, changing the subject. 'They were better than last year.'

Last year Nick had gone to see the fireworks with Carolyn. All he remembered was the argument they'd had on the bus on the way home.

'There was a riot on Bondi Beach,' said Sally. 'Mostly English backpackers, according to the radio. They were fighting pitched battles with the police outside the Pavilion. It sounded pretty ugly.'

Nick picked up the paper – having the *Daily Star* delivered free every morning was one of the few staff benefits that hadn't been axed in the last round of cost-cutting. The front page was filled with pictures of fireworks bursting over the Harbour Bridge. Nick turned to page three. There was nothing about British hooligans running amok on Bondi Beach. 'So where's this riot, then?'

'It must have happened too late for the second edition. Rioters have no respect for deadlines.'

Compared with previous years, the harbour celebrations had gone off quietly. The *Star* had photographs of two policemen dancing with revellers in The Rocks, and of a police horse wearing a party hat. But the new year had delivered its usual list of casualties: victims of drunken brawls and exploding fireworks; a late-night fisherman swept off the rocks at Garie Beach, a middle-aged man killed in a hit-and-run in Randwick; a mother and child missing from a yacht in Pittwater.

Sally glanced out of the window. 'Do you think it's hungry?'

'The dog? Probably.'

'What do dogs eat?'

'I thought you were going to ring the pound.'

'I am. But it's a public holiday, remember? We can hardly starve it until tomorrow.'

'There'll be something at the shop,' said Nick, looking for his wallet. 'I'll go and buy him something.'

'It's a she.'

'Sorry?'

'The dog you seem to know so much about. It's a she. Only a minor detail, I know, but I thought you might have noticed.'

Nick took out his cigarettes. 'Minor details often escape me.'

In the old days, when Sydney still had rival afternoon papers, there were two hotels on neighbouring corners of Broadway: the broadsheet *Herald* journalists patronised one and the tabloid *Sun* hacks crowded into the other. At night, groups of printers stood around a spluttering brazier on the wedge-shaped island in the middle of Wattle Street. Nick's father had worked at the *Sun*, in the circulations department. Nick remembered him coming home each evening and slapping down his free copy of the late edition on the kitchen table, as if it was his own byline on the front-page splash.

Walking along Abercrombie Street towards Broadway, Nick caught the pungent whiff of fermenting hops from the Carlton brewery. While he waited for the traffic lights to change, he watched a semitrailer loaded with giant rolls of newsprint backing into the *Herald*'s receiving bay. In a couple of years the presses would move to a greenfields site out west and the area would begin its metamorphosis into a pseudo-village of red-brick townhouses and warehouse conversions. But for the time being the newsprint kept coming, arriving in rolls and departing in bundles. The pedestrian light flashed green as the semitrailer's red cab withdrew, like the head of a tortoise, into the receiving bay.

Nick wasn't due at work until six. Emerging from the pedestrian tunnel, he climbed Devonshire Street and turned left into Crown, retracing his walk from the previous night. He knew where he was going but not why. He'd seen Danny off his face at the club, and he'd seen Danny's car, abandoned but recently driven – presumably by Danny. What did he hope to gain by knowing more?

He kept on walking. Crown Street on Sunday evening was mostly deserted. He crossed the road and walked another couple of blocks. A lime-green kombivan was illegally parked at the entrance to the cobbled lane where he'd seen Danny's car. An acrid smell caught his nostrils: the smell of scorched metal.

Two teenagers in jackets and beanies were huddled beside the kombivan doing some kind of deal. Nick looked past them into the lane – and saw the charred body of the metallic blue Audi TT standing in a puddle of oily water. He hesitated a moment before approaching.

Amid the incinerated wreckage it was easy to see the empty space below the dashboard where the sound system had once been. A crystalline mound of toughened-glass fragments lay on the back seat, just inside the door, although the front and rear windscreens had clearly been blown outwards when the fuel tank exploded. Somebody had broken into the Audi by smashing a side window and then stolen the stereo. Either the thief or someone else had set the car alight.

*　　*　　*

Tuesday was Sally's day off. She and Jess had spent the morning splashing each other in the kids' pool in Victoria Park. Nick, meanwhile, was doing his best to bath the dog in the laundry sink.

At the sound of the animal barking, Jess came running down the hall. She stood in the doorway and said, 'Mummy's wet her pants.'

Nick was still getting used to the room-silencing confessions that could fall from the mouth of a three-year-old. 'Really?'

'She did it at the pool.'

'That's a shame.'

'I seed her do it.'

'Saw,' said Nick.

'I sawed her do it.'

'I don't know what she's telling you,' said Sally, shutting the door behind her.

'I don't think you want to,' said Nick.

'Whatever it is, it's not absolutely necessary to believe it.'

'That's what I was hoping.'

She stopped at the entrance to the kitchen. Nick had put too much shampoo in the water and the cracked linoleum floor was covered in suds. 'Can I ask what you think you're doing?'

'I think I'm washing the dog.' He paused. 'I might be washing the floor.'

'Why?'

'Why what?'

'Why are you washing the dog?'

'She's been living rough. She needs it.'

'I thought we decided you were going to ring the pound.'

'I thought we decided you were.'

Jess crouched down in front of the greyhound and said, 'You mustn't get suds in his ears.'

'She's a girl dog, Jess,' said Nick. 'And I'm being very careful not to get suds in her ears.'

'I don't like suds in my ears,' said Jess.

'How are you going to rinse it?' asked Sally.

Nick stopped lathering the dog's coat and wiped his hands on a towel. 'I haven't thought that far ahead. Maybe a hose in the yard . . . ?'

Sally's eyes narrowed. 'Are you trying to soften me up?'

'Why would I try to do that?'

'Jess knows I don't have time to look after a dog. I've promised her a guinea pig when she's five.'

'A guinea pig?'

'When she's five.'

'Well, that's something to look forward to.' He smiled doubtfully at Jess. 'Isn't it, Jess?'

Sally frowned. 'I wouldn't expect you to know this, Nick, but three is generally considered too young to appreciate irony.'

'What if I looked after her?' Nick suggested. 'After all, I was the one she followed home. If it doesn't work out, I'll ring the pound.'

Sally studied him, as though trying to identify the subtle physical change that signalled the transformation from unencumbered single urban male to domesticated dog-owner. 'Is this because of Carolyn?' she asked.

'Carolyn never let me hose her down in the backyard,' Nick said.

There was a long silence.

'She won't sleep in the house,' said Nick. 'I'll buy a plastic kennel.'

'I suppose you've given it a name.'

'I haven't. But Jess has. She wants to call her Fred.'

She smiled at Jess. 'Fred isn't really a girl's name, darling.'

'She's not a girl,' said Jess. 'She's a dog.'

It was Thursday evening. Nick was struggling to think of a clever headline for a wire story about an alligator running amok in the suburbs of Tupelo. The tagline at the bottom was from the *Daily Mississippian*. What on earth, Nick wondered, was the *Star* doing reprinting stories from the *Daily Mississippian* – in fact what was anyone doing reprinting stories from the *Daily Mississippian*? Once upon a time the *Star* had taken its international news from the *New York Post*, London's *Daily Mirror*; sometimes even the tacky *Bild Zeitung*; now it was filching paragraphs from the *Daily Mississippian* and the *Waco Tribune-Herald*.

He skim-read to the end. Most of the jokes that sprang readily to mind for a rampaging alligator story were already there in the copy. As a last resort Nick knew he could always steal the best joke and delete it from the story. But Jerry Whistler, the chief sub, had read the raw copy and would know straight away what he'd done. Jerry was one of the few people in the newsroom Nick found it hard to get along with. And Jerry was one of Sally's drinking buddies. There was a photograph of the two of them on Sally's fridge, hamming it up a couple of years ago on the subs' Christmas cruise. How did these things happen, Nick used to ask himself, as he watched Jerry Whistler hammering away at his keyboard like some demented church organist. How could Sally be friends with both of them?

As if he knew what Nick was thinking, Jerry looked up from his screen. Jerry had a lazy eye. To compensate he tended to squint with the other, screwing up the left side of his face as though taking aim through an imaginary gun sight. The wire basket on top of Jerry's computer screen was empty, which meant all that night's foreign stories had been assigned. For most of the past hour Jerry had been scrolling idly through the local news directory, pretending to be busy, when all he was doing was saving himself the trouble of having to read the paper in the morning.

'Looks like your mate Grogan has got himself in a bit of strife,' he said.

Nick could see Jerry Whistler waiting for him to react.

'Let me guess,' he said. 'The Crypt has been raided again. Grogan's been watering the beer.'

'Not quite. It seems that young Danny has been a naughty boy behind the wheel.'

Nick felt a shiver go through him.

'New Year's Eve,' said Jerry. 'A camera caught him doing ninety down Moore Park Road.'

'Who got the story?'

'Flynn,' replied Jerry.

It usually took at least a fortnight for a speeding notice to grind its way through the system. But Danny Grogan wasn't your ordinary speeding driver. If Flynn had the story then someone in the police media liaison unit must have been shooting his mouth off. But how had the police found out? Fixed speed cameras were the responsibility of the Roads and

Transport Authority. The police only became involved if the notice was challenged and the matter went to court. Danny Grogan was a prize scalp. Someone had spotted Danny's name and made a few calls.

All Nick knew about Michael Flynn, the new crime reporter, was what he'd read on the staff noticeboard: Flynn was a lawyer who'd been a political adviser to the New South Wales police minister before taking a 75 percent pay cut to join the *Star*, and that he was fluent in Mandarin. Fifteen – even ten – years ago a *Daily Star* reporter was borderline overqualified if they knew how to use an apostrophe and could name the prime minister of New Zealand. Flynn would be editor before he was thirty-five.

Nick called up the story and read it as he waited for the foreign page proofs to arrive. At 10.27 p.m. on New Year's Eve a metallic blue Audi TT with the registration number CR1PT had been caught by a speed camera doing ninety-three kilometres an hour on Moore Park Road.

The rest of the story – another ten paragraphs and a selection of incriminating pictures from the files – consisted of a potted summary of the troubled life of Danny Grogan, including a list of previous driving offences. Nick didn't have to read the list to know that it was only eighteen months since Danny had been caught drink-driving outside the Bat and Ball Hotel. Thanks to some expensive legal representation Danny had escaped with a suspended sentence but the magistrate had made it clear that another conviction would mean jail.

Flynn's information sounded good but none of the quotes were attributed, which meant that whoever had spoken to Flynn knew they were breaking the rules. At this time of night, as Nick knew only too well, it was almost impossible to reach anyone on the phone. You checked as many details as you could and either ran with what you had or held off and risked a bollocking at the morning news conference when the story turned up in the *Herald*.

Still, Nick knew a few things that Flynn didn't. He knew, for a start, what state Danny Grogan had been in on New Year's Eve. And, for what it was worth, he knew that Danny wasn't alone that night. Not that he intended to share that information with Flynn. The whole thing looked suspiciously like the sort of off-the-record media stunt that had got the New South Wales police into trouble over the years. It reminded Nick of the choreographed drug swoops and stage-managed arrests so adored by TV news bulletins – and so skilfully exploited by defence barristers when the matter came to court.

In dealing with the police it was important, Nick had discovered, never to underestimate their capacity for duplicity. Experience had taught him to follow a simple rule: assume the police have something to hide (which is not necessarily what they are hiding) and ask questions accordingly. Michael Flynn, for all his fluent Mandarin, had only been the *Star*'s crime reporter for a few weeks – not long enough to have developed an instinct for when the police media unit might be over-selling a story.

The storm broke shortly after Nick got home from work. It began as a fierce, dry wind rattling the windows in their frames. Then it stopped. Thunder crackled in the distance but it seemed to be moving away, not coming closer. The noise Nick heard next was like a car wheel spinning in gravel. It erupted out of nowhere. Then there were lumps of hail bouncing off the tin roof. The dog was barking in her kennel. Through the gap beneath the door Nick saw the landing light go on. He heard Sally go into Jess's room. If he knew anything about Jess, it was her mother who would be more frightened.

He thought about Danny. If he'd been stopped by a booze bus rather than picked up by a speed camera, the police would have found out he had the contents of a chemistry lab coursing around his system. Things could have been a lot worse for Danny. But they were bad enough.

Outside, the dog was howling. Lightning flashed behind the curtains. Nick went downstairs, slipped the bolts at the top and bottom of the kitchen door and whistled to the dog. Bounding out of the darkness, the greyhound shot past him, skittering sideways across the linoleum floor until it bounced with a hollow thud off the pantry door. Nick wondered what to do next.

Wondering what to do next was something Nick found himself doing a lot these days. Not about Carolyn: that was over. Maybe they would come out of it as friends. Nick didn't mind the idea of giving it a try once the dust had settled. No, wondering what to do next was about more than finding someone to replace Carolyn. It was about finding someone to replace the person he'd been while he and Carolyn were together. That person already felt oddly remote. Perhaps it had something to do with the amount of time they had been together. Before Carolyn, Nick's romantic history had been strictly short-term. He had friends at the paper who'd met, married and divorced within the space of eighteen months. It was going to take some time for him to adjust to not being the person he was.

The greyhound inclined its slipper-shaped skull to one side, its eyes bulging hopefully, and after a moment's hesitation

Nick followed the animal upstairs, where it spent the night curled up among the shoes at the bottom of his wardrobe.

The phone was ringing: in Nick's mind. It seemed to ring for hours before a familiar voice swam up from the depths. 'Telephone, Nick. For you.'

His alarm had failed to go off, because Nick had failed to set it. He stumbled downstairs and picked up the receiver.

'Nicolas?'

He didn't recognise the voice.

'This is Harry Grogan. We met some years ago.'

'Yes,' said Nick, vaguely remembering a surreal encounter outside the huge wrought-iron gates of the Grogan mansion.

'Have you read the papers?'

'No,' said Nick, although he guessed what the call was going to be about.

'Danny's been caught speeding.'

Nick didn't say anything. As far as driving offences went, Danny was on his last life.

'I'd like to talk to you, Nicolas. See if there's anything that can be done.'

'What Danny needs is a lawyer, Mr Grogan.'

'I'd still like to talk to you.'

There was a sharpness in the older man's voice, a hard edge beneath the courtesy that Nick had heard many times before: at shareholder meetings, as Grogan brushed off annoying questions about directors' remuneration; at press conferences, while slapping down half-hearted interrogations about zoning restrictions or endangered butterflies. Harry Grogan was accustomed to being obeyed.

'I really don't see how I can help,' said Nick.

'I'll send a car for you,' said Grogan.

'I'm working this afternoon.'

'This won't take long, Nicolas.'

'All right. I suppose . . .'

'I knew you wouldn't let me down.'

Nick was just getting into the shower when there was a knock at the front door. Sally's voice shouted up the stairs, 'Someone for you, Nick.'

Harry Grogan must have sent the chauffeur even before picking up the phone. Nick wondered how Grogan had known where to find him. Someone on the switchboard must have broken the rules by giving out his address. He had asked for a silent number after a series of anonymous calls to the flat he'd shared with Carolyn in Elizabeth Bay. For a while the police had put an intercept on his phone at work. The anonymous calls stopped without Nick finding out who was behind them or what they were about – or whether they were even intended for him. For all he knew, the calls could have been meant for Carolyn. As a criminal lawyer she had no shortage of intimidating clients. But Nick had stopped being the *Star*'s crime reporter a year ago. Now he was a subeditor on the foreign news desk. Subeditors on the foreign news desk didn't need protecting from anyone – except themselves, maybe.

Harry Grogan's chauffeur was tanned and stocky, with an inverted saucer of black hair on the crown of his head that reminded Nick of the black-helmeted birds he saw wading in the ponds in Centennial Park. His broad shoulders and bulging biceps looked like the product of long daily workouts in front

of a mirror. Nick guessed he was in his late fifties or early sixties
– too old, he couldn't help thinking, for a body like that.

Sitting there, half wet from his half shower, Nick soon realised
that the Jaguar was heading not for the marble cylinder beside
the botanical gardens that formed the headquarters of Grogan
Constructions, but for the slip road to the Harbour Bridge.

'Where are we going?' he asked. 'I thought I'd be meeting
Mr Grogan in his office.'

'Mr Grogan is at his vineyard today.'

'I start work at five.'

'Mr Grogan has instructed me to have you back here by 4.45.'

Nick knew all about the vineyard. While Grogan
Constructions was busy ripping up 100-year-old Moreton Bay
fig trees, Danny's father used to have himself photographed
among the trellises in his olive-green gumboots and Driza-
Bone coat. With its organic vineyard and rammed-earth tasting
room, and its ostentatious donations to WWF, Grogan Estate
Wines was a badge of environmental respectability for a
company that stood for its opposite. Harry Grogan had even
succeeded in luring a busload of wine journalists to the Hunter
Valley to watch him roll up his trousers and crush grapes
between his toes. That was the thing about Grogan: he knew
that if you told one story well enough, journalists would eventually stop asking you about all the other stories.

The windows of the Jaguar were so heavily tinted that it
could have been evening outside. Harry Grogan's cars had
always been dark – and English. Nick remembered the claret-
coloured Daimler that waited for Danny outside the school
gates on the rare evenings when his presence was required
at home. And he remembered Danny's little jokes about the

'weirdo' chauffeur who wore leather driving gloves, even in the middle of summer.

'Nice gloves,' said Nick.

The chauffeur said nothing but reached across to switch on the radio.

The stock market was falling but Grogan Constructions was having a good morning, up nearly 5 percent in the first few minutes of trade. There was speculation in the *Herald* that Harry Grogan was ready to sign a deal with the Consolidated Gaming Company of Illinois to build a Dreamland casino in Las Vegas and, at the same time, that Grogan was close to reaching agreement with a Dutch company to develop a luxury Dreamland resort on the French Polynesian island of Bora Bora. Before long, the company boasted, there would be a Dreamland on every continent.

Harry Grogan was a master at bypassing the orthodox institutional channels and talking straight to the media, putting the day traders in a frenzy for a session or two while the stock exchange timidly sought 'clarification' of the rumours.

There was a grim irony, Nick used to think, that a company founded on concrete should trade so heavily in gossip, but it had been that way from the beginning.

The very name Dreamland evoked dark rumours about the blaze that had destroyed the rotting Edwardian amusement park two decades ago. Three street kids had died in the Tunnel of Love, their names memorialised in a children's charity generously funded by the Grogan Foundation.

Speculation about the cause of the fire, fuelled by a fat insurance payout and by the local council's decision not to allow the park to be rebuilt, had dogged Harry Grogan ever since. But Grogan wasn't the only developer benefiting from insurance fires in Sydney during the 1980s. Keeping the Dreamland name was either an act of monstrous hubris or of clumsy atonement; the media had never been sure which.

There was still the odd ratbag, of course, like the old man in shabby coat and shiny trousers, father of one of the dead children, who used to disrupt press conferences by shouting questions about the Dreamland fire – but these days the ratbags rarely made it onto the evening news bulletins. If there was something rank beneath the foundations of Harry Grogan's harbourside citadel, Sydney didn't want to know about it.

For the few eccentrics (American widows on cruise ships, the occasional lone yachtsman) who still came to Australia by sea, Dreamland was their first sight of the continent, a glittering steel-and-marble monolith rising seven storeys above the harbour on the site where the creaking timber roller-coaster had rattled and roared since the 1920s.

Inside the atrium stood the tallest pot plant in the southern hemisphere, a Canary Islands Date Palm (*Phoenix canariensis*) only a few metres shorter than the great Chilean Wine Palm (*Jubaea chilensis*) at the Temperate House in Kew Gardens. Asked by a journalist what he would do when the date palm grew too tall for the atrium, Harry Grogan had smiled and replied that he would chop it down and plant something smaller.

Nick had been among the crowd that day, a cadet reporter in an uncomfortable suit sent to pester the suntanned socialites swarming over the newly opened hotel in hopes of getting their picture taken with Billy Joel. Danny Grogan, not surprisingly, had refused to be anywhere near the site of his father's triumph. His mother had floated in the background: a slim, sorrowful-looking figure in a wide-brimmed hat clutching a permanently half-full champagne flute. According to Danny they had stopped sleeping in the same room while he was still in his cot and by the time he was at school could barely stand to be in the same house together. Her expression that day was something Nick had never forgotten – a steely rejection of the celebrations going on around her and a silent avowal that, whatever it might be to her husband, this wasn't her idea of Dreamland.

Two hours after leaving Sydney, the Jaguar swung off the road onto a gravel track that wound through the vineyards to the rammed-earth building with GROGAN ESTATE WINES painted in black letters on its corrugated iron roof.

Harry Grogan stood in the doorway, the pinstriped boardroom megalomaniac rather unconvincingly dressed in lumberjack shirt, corduroy trousers and olive-green Wellingtons.

'Nicolas. It was good of you to come.'

'I don't think I had a choice, did I?'

They shook hands. 'One always has a choice, Nicolas.'

'I'd assumed we would meet in the city.'

Grogan smiled and ushered him inside. 'Never assume anything. That's a rule I've always followed, Nicolas. Assumptions have a tendency to be misplaced.'

'I'll remember that.'

The room was much bigger than it promised from outside. Light flooded through big north-facing windows. The wall behind the tasting counter was covered with diamond-shaped wine racks. Other walls were decorated with plaques and awards. In the centre of the room stood a rustic table, already laid for lunch, and two high-backed chairs.

It was just after eleven o'clock. 'I thought we might have something to eat,' said Grogan, gesturing towards a chair. 'I hope you're hungry.'

'Listen, Mr Grogan. If this is about doing something for Danny—'

The older man cut him off. 'He always liked you, Nicolas.'

The possibility suddenly occurred to Nick that Danny might be somewhere near, waiting for the right moment to show himself. 'Was calling me Danny's idea?'

'Danny doesn't know I've spoken to you. He thinks he can sort this out by himself.' Grogan smiled. 'My son has always had an exaggerated impression of his independence. You know it was my money that bought the nightclub?'

Nick thought for a few moments before speaking. 'It was a disused church when you bought it, Mr Grogan. Danny turned it into a nightclub.'

'I admire your loyalty, Nicolas. Deluded as it probably is.'

A middle-aged woman emerged from a red door behind the tasting counter, carrying a plate of antipasto. Without looking at her, Grogan said, 'Thank you, Estelle.' He picked up the bottle of Grogan Estate pinot noir that was standing in the middle of the table. 'You'll have some wine?'

'Why not?'

Danny's father poured two large glasses. 'Tell me what you know.'

'About Danny?'

'Isn't that why we're here?'

'I know what I read in the paper,' said Nick. 'A camera caught Danny speeding on Moore Park Road.'

'Is that all?'

It was obvious that Danny's father knew more. 'Pretty much,' he said.

'You know Danny is serving a suspended sentence?'

'Yes.'

'If he's convicted of another offence he'll go to jail.'

Nick didn't say anything. Danny had been lucky until now but his luck had run out. Some people never had any luck to begin with. Maybe Danny deserved what was coming to him.

'Danny's mother is under sedation, Nicolas.'

Nick had never met Mrs Grogan face-to-face. She was as reclusive as her husband was ubiquitous. Apart from a handful taken at the Dreamland opening, the only picture in the *Star*'s photographic library was nearly fifteen years old: the developer's wife in silk headscarf, white raincoat and dark glasses scurrying into a Paddington boutique. The shot reminded Nick of Jackie Onassis – or Princess Diana. As a child Danny rarely spoke about his mother. Nick had the impression she was often ill. Of course the rumours of her husband's infidelities couldn't have helped. If the gossip was true, Harry Grogan had a whole harem of mistresses installed in penthouse units around the city. None of the mistresses had ever come forward, of course. Still, it wasn't hard to see why Mrs Grogan shunned the public gaze.

'I'm sorry.'

'It would kill her if Danny went to jail.'

'If you want me to speak on Danny's behalf in court,' said Nick, 'I'll do it.'

'That's kind of you, Nicolas. But it's not exactly what I was thinking of.'

'What were you thinking of?'

Danny's father picked up his glass and swirled it around, his eyes fixed on the wine. Half a minute passed before he lifted his gaze. 'I want you to say you were driving Danny's car.'

'That's absurd,' said Nick. 'They have him on camera.'

'They have the car on camera. It was nearly midnight. In such cases, I'm told, it is all but impossible to identify the driver.'

'Why should I have been driving Danny's car? And if I was driving Danny's car, why would I have been doing ninety kilometres an hour on Moore Park Road? I know that road. There are speed cameras all over the place.' He paused. 'No, Mr Grogan. I'm sorry. It's a crazy idea. I'd like to help Danny but . . . not like this.'

Grogan waited for some time before speaking again. 'Danny will nominate you as the driver at the time of the accident. He will say you offered to drive him home. At some point he changed his mind and asked you to take him back to the nightclub. All you have to do, Nicolas, is agree. Danny's lawyer will obtain a formal statement to that effect. The case against Danny will be dismissed. I believe I'm right in saying that you have recently experienced the break-up of a long-term relationship. The magistrate will take into account your emotional state at the time of the incident, together with the fact that it happened on New Year's Eve, and let you off with a fine.'

Nick studied his face over the table. 'You're not joking, are you?'

'No, Nicolas. I'm not joking.'

'What makes you think the police will believe I was driving the car?'

'Can you suggest any reason they might have for not believing you?'

'I'd be committing perjury,' said Nick. 'I could end up in jail.'

'Nobody would be able to prove it,' said Grogan. 'Not if you were careful. Not if you stuck to your story.'

Nick thought about the sequined handbag he'd seen in the front seat of the Audi. 'Someone was with Danny that night. A girl.'

Grogan's expression hardened. 'Danny was alone, Nicolas. He wasn't with anyone.'

'No, Mr Grogan. I'm sorry Danny's in trouble. But I'm not getting mixed up in this.' A few seconds passed before Nick heard himself say, 'It's not worth the risk.' Those last few words took him by surprise – as if they had been spoken by someone else. 'What I mean is, it's too dangerous. For Danny as well as me. Lying will only get Danny into more trouble than he's in already.'

'Danny has always been a good liar,' Grogan said. 'It's the one thing I can always trust him to do.'

Nick didn't say anything.

Grogan finished his wine and cradled the empty glass in his hand. 'What do you think the risk is worth?'

'I beg your pardon.'

'A few moments ago you said that doing this little favour for Danny wasn't worth the risk.'

'So?'

'So, I'm asking you what would make it worth the risk?'

'What are you talking about?'

'You know what I'm talking about, Nicolas. You're an intelligent man. And like an intelligent man, you're pretending not to know.'

'You've lost me, Mr Grogan. I thought we were talking about helping Danny.'

'We are.' The older man paused. 'I'm just waiting for you to tell me the price.'

'The price?'

'*Your* price.'

'I'm not with you.'

'Of course you are. The course of action I'm urging carries a degree of risk. It's only fair to put a price on that risk. I'm asking you to name the price.'

'In terms of what?'

'In terms of money, Nicolas.'

'This is ridiculous.'

'Is it?'

'You think money will persuade me to lie for Danny?'

'Isn't that why you're here?'

Nick hesitated. 'No,' he said. 'Of course not.'

'Come on, Nicolas. You must have some idea. Twenty thousand? Fifty? A hundred thousand? Would it be worth a hundred thousand dollars to you to tell the police you got carried away by the excitement of driving Danny's car and broke the speed limit?'

Grogan made it sound trivial – a game almost, like stealing traffic cones or defacing road signs. Maybe it was a game, Nick thought. After all, nobody had been hurt. Nick thought about the money. A hundred thousand dollars was roughly ninety-five thousand more than he'd managed to save after a decade of full-time employment. He thought about the timing. He'd left the Judgment Bar around 10 p.m. and stood outside the Supreme Court for a while smoking a cigarette before deciding to try his luck at the Crypt. The speed camera had clocked Danny's Audi at 10.27 p.m. on Moore Park Road. Between leaving the Judgment Bar and joining the queue outside the nightclub just before 11 p.m., he hadn't spoken to a soul.

Nick waited a long time before answering. Once he might have said yes without thinking. He might even have felt he owed it to Danny, as a friend, to give him the alibi he needed. Maybe, deep down, he still felt that. Or maybe he didn't. He thought about the money. He thought about himself thinking about the money. The money wasn't his idea. It wasn't as though he'd asked for it. Maybe, after all, he would have done this thing for Danny without the money. Maybe.

'I'll think about it,' said Nick. 'I'm not promising anything.'

Grogan scribbled a mobile phone number on a lined page torn from his diary. 'In case you need to call me.'

Nick glanced at the last four digits – 7777 – before folding the page and slipping it in his pocket.

Looking at Danny's father, Nick knew that the last thirty minutes had been a charade: of patience and humility on Grogan's side, and of integrity, or at least discretion, on his. If he hesitated it was because he wasn't sure of being able to pull off his side of the bargain. He could imagine lying impulsively – or even cunningly and deliberately – to save his own skin. In fact he didn't need to imagine it. He'd done it countless times, in greater or lesser ways. But what would it take to stand up in court and perjure himself – to coolly take the blame for something he hadn't done?

41

He watched Harry Grogan put out his hand and he watched himself take it. For an instant he had the weird sensation that this wasn't him, that the person shaking Grogan's hand was a stranger. He used to get the same feeling on death-knocks, speaking to the parents of teenage boys who'd driven into power poles or jumped in front of trains: the momentary feeling of not recognising himself, of listening to a voice that wasn't his, of knowing and somehow not knowing what he was doing there. There was something hard and sarcastic in Grogan's smile, as if he knew exactly what Nick was thinking, as if he'd witnessed such moral spasms before and always seen them overcome.

'You'll need to speak to Danny's solicitor. His name is Roy Bellamy. He's expecting your call.'

After leaving the circulations department of the *Sun*, Nick's father had taken a job in insurance. He became an adjuster: he adjusted people's claims to fit their losses. Nick's father understood loss and the effects of loss – grief, anger, the need to recover what was not recoverable. He was generous in his adjustments. He liked to think of himself as fair, although fairness was not his business.

Mr Carmody was well known in Sydney's hailstorm belt: a balding cheerful little man who never said no to a cup of tea. And further afield, in flood-prone towns up north and hamlets in the Blue Mountains where bushfires raged every few years. Nick had seen photographs of his father standing in his shirt-sleeves among the ashes of burnt-out homes; bending down among the charred timbers to rescue a brooch or a teapot. People still spoke of him in Bellingen, Taree, Mount Victoria, Medlow Bath, towns famous for their disasters. He was the fellow who arrived in the wake of hailstorms and whirlwinds and set about putting a price on what was lost.

Nick thought of him as he sat in the Jaguar, watching the scenery fly past the darkened windows. His father had never accepted a dollar he hadn't earned. But the world had changed. In his father's day money was the means of acquiring essentials: a car, a house, a two-week holiday at the coast every summer. Now money was the essence, and Nick felt the lack of it. By Harry Grogan's standards a hundred thousand dollars wasn't a big sum, but it felt like a big sum to Nick – enough to change his life. When the driver handed him a small package from the Jaguar's glove box, he took it.

It was 2.15 p.m. as Nick climbed the steps from Town Hall station. He had an hour to kill before his meeting with Roy Bellamy. There was a big red 'Sale' sticker in the window of the Rubicon bookshop. The Rubicon was where Nick and Carolyn had met – upstairs, among the second-hand shelves. Nick had lost count of the afternoons they had spent in the coffee shop, reading books they had no intention of buying, and afterwards buying books they had no prospect of reading.

He went inside. The upstairs section was even more cluttered than usual. Scattered around the walls were hundreds of distressed paperbacks: concave airport thrillers and dog-eared romances bought by the kilogram or by the metre and displayed in pink plastic baskets, like offal in a Chinese market.

Near the window overlooking the street was a trestle table marked 'Crime'. Nick circled the table, picking up books and then putting them back: long-out-of-print detective novels by Fergus Hume and Frederic Dannay; obscure psychological thrillers by Frances Iles; the odd Father Brown mystery, smelling of must and Mortein. This was the sort of literature Nick liked to read, the sort he wished he had the talent to write.

Among the leaning towers of broken-spined paperbacks were publishers' remainders and dumped foreign editions, never opened, let alone read. These held no interest for Nick. There was something abject, he thought, about an unread book in a second-hand bookshop. He picked up a well-thumbed Simenon and took it downstairs to the counter.

Roy Bellamy had rooms in Macquarie Street overlooking the Mint in a building pregnant with obstetricians. He was a short fleshy man with a comb-over that looked as if it had been painted on with a calligrapher's brush.

The solicitor waited for his elderly secretary to close the door before signalling for Nick to sit down. 'Mr Carmody,' he said. 'Thank you for coming.'

After shaking hands Bellamy removed his glasses and began polishing the lenses with a corner of his white cotton handkerchief.

'Are you related to George Carmody, by any chance?'

'Not that I'm aware of.'

'I'm relieved to hear it.'

'Who's George Carmody?'

'He's a barrister. An unscrupulous one. I had a fleeting suspicion that you looked like him.' He replaced his glasses and steepled his plump fingers on the desk. 'You've come forward, I understand, to give evidence on behalf of Daniel Grogan.'

The formal way he said it made Nick suspect for a moment that Bellamy might be recording the conversation.

'Are you taping this?' he asked.

'Would it matter if I was?'

'It might.'

Bellamy smiled and produced a small tape-recorder from the top drawer of his desk. Nick could see that the spools were not turning. 'Satisfied?' Bellamy studied him across the table. 'You're the man who tracked down Mr Milhench.'

Nick shrugged. 'It didn't do me much good.'

'Don't undervalue yourself. Mr Milhench and I have had intermittent professional dealings over the years. I'd have to say he is one of the more ingenious criminals I've had the pleasure of representing.'

'It was a lucky tip,' said Nick. 'It could just as easily have gone to someone else.'

'But it went to you.'

'Yes.'

The solicitor took off his glasses. The act of polishing them seemed to clarify his thoughts. 'In my experience, Mr Carmody, life rarely happens by accident. The purpose is not always obvious, I admit. But luck seldom offers a satisfactory explanation.'

Nick didn't speak. He hadn't come here for a philosophical discussion. His own experience, at any rate, told him exactly the opposite: most of the time luck offered the only explanation.

Bellamy put the glasses back on his face. 'You and Daniel have known each other for a long time?'

'About twenty years.'

'Old friends.'

Nick wondered whether the solicitor knew that he was only here because he was being paid. He remembered something a criminal barrister had once told him: a good lawyer never asks a question to which he doesn't wish to know the answer.

'You understand,' said Bellamy, 'that I am acting as Daniel's solicitor. You have been brought to my attention as a material witness to an incident involving my client. Daniel has informed me that you were the person driving his car when it was photographed speeding on Moore Park Road on the night of New Year's Eve. If you are prepared to corroborate Daniel's statement then I am prepared to advise a course of action. Is that why you are here?'

'That's why I'm here.'

'The court will require a signed statement explaining how you came to be driving Daniel's car at the time the offence was committed. Are you willing to provide that?'

'Just tell me what to write.'

Nick had expected the case to be dealt with summarily: a summary admission of guilt followed by a summary punishment. But the police smelt a rat. They had a confession but it wasn't the one they wanted. Now Nick was frightened. Danny's case would go to court, with Nick as the principal witness. The prosecution would try to catch him out. The process had probably started already. Somebody would be checking Nicolas Carmody's driving record, his criminal record – they might even investigate his mobile phone records. Thank Christ he hadn't made any attempt to contact Danny.

It was too late to back out. He couldn't withdraw his statement without admitting to perjury. Besides, there was the money. The money made it conspiracy to pervert the course of justice. So far all he'd taken was the five thousand dollars in cash given to him by Grogan's chauffeur. The envelope, opened and hurriedly re-sealed, was sitting in the bottom drawer of a locked grey filing cabinet at work – a radioactive presence he could feel glowing in the corner of the news-room. It was the safest place he could think to hide it, buried beneath piles of notebooks. No cleaner had gone near those filing cabinets for years – decades, even. An air of cultish superstition hung over them. There were locked drawers belonging to reporters who'd left the paper, who'd been sacked, who'd died. A drawer, once assigned, could never be reassigned. The faded name tags were like a memorial. If you dug deep enough you'd find shorthand notes of interviews with every prime minister since Menzies.

Sitting by himself in the staff canteen, picking at a Caesar salad consisting of nothing but iceberg lettuce and mayon-naise, Nick read about an amateur skydiver in Sauk City, Wisconsin who fell twelve thousand feet into a suburban carpark, suffering only bruised ribs, a fractured collar bone and a broken jaw. Passers-by watched in horror as the skydiver hurtled silently out of a cloudless sky and landed face-down on the tarmac. According to *Real Life* magazine, Laura-May Holmes lay rigid for several seconds before realising that she was still alive, then sat up and asked for a drink of water.

Roy Bellamy was wrong. At some elemental level, Nick knew, survival was purely a matter of chance. If his father had driven a single kilometre per hour faster for the last forty-five minutes of his life, then the semitrailer that swung across the road, killing him and Nick's mother, would have slid harmlessly into a ditch.

Nick remembered, at twenty-one, stepping carelessly between two parked cars, hearing the blast of a horn and the rush of air as a delivery van hurtled by, centimetres from his face. Had he stepped out a fraction further, or had the delivery van been travelling a fraction faster, his short career at the *Daily Star* would have been over.

Two years later, as he stood outside the Glebe Coroner's Court, a butcher's van had left the road and struck a bus shelter, killing an old man from whom Nick had just cadged a cigarette.

Twelve years at the *Daily Star* had given Nick a pragmatic view of life. He had seen too much evidence of the randomness of misfortune to believe in fate or predestination or just deserts. Journalism reinforced his gut belief that life just happened, that any attempt to draw a moral or extract a meaning was futile.

Nick remembered being sent, as a fresh-faced cadet, to interview the tearful widow of a man who'd drowned in his backyard swimming pool after apparently being attacked by his next-door neighbour's pitbull terrier. The headline was MAN DROWNS AFTER FIGHT WITH KILLER DOG. The following day Nick was sent back to speak to the dead man's daughter, who swore that the pitbull had in fact been trying to pull the drowning man from the pool.

The next morning's headline was HERO DOG'S FIGHT TO SAVE DROWNING MAN. The *Daily Star* even used the same grainy photograph for both stories, taken with a disposable camera from a nearby block of units. According to the remorseless logic of the midday news conference, the second story didn't negate the first, it just superseded (and perhaps even improved) it. Of course by then the unfortunate animal had already been put down, but Nick's story didn't mention that.

In the newsroom of the *Daily Star* Nick had achieved a

kind of fame as author of the 'dead dog yarn', but Nick himself had been too embarrassed to own up to it, even to Carolyn.

As a reporter Nick wanted to believe that truth mattered, that truth was the one thing that did matter. Lying to save Danny Grogan from prison went against everything he stood for as a journalist – and yet, he reflected, it probably wasn't the worst lie he'd ever told. He'd told bigger lies and convinced himself they had been necessary to get the story – and perhaps they had. He wished he'd turned down the money, forgetting for a moment that money was his reason for doing it. It was funny how you could make yourself forget a thing like that. Would he have taken the money if he and Carolyn had still been together? He didn't know the answer to that.

The press outside Central Local Court were more numerous than the pigeons. Nick knew half of them by name: Stuart Scullion from the *Star* and his brother Barry from the *Herald*, Sue Garfield and Keith Eddy from Australian Associated Press, plus reporters from 702 and most of the commercial radio stations, and crews from the four television networks, drinking takeaway coffee and checking the batteries in their tape-recorders.

Somehow, in the weeks that Nick had had to prepare for Danny Grogan's trial, he'd managed to convince himself that this was going to be a private affair. He'd never had more than a casual conversation with Scullion in the canteen queue but he nodded anyway and said, 'G'day Stuart.'

'Nick,' said Scullion, detaching himself briefly from the scrum. 'Don't say they've got you covering this?'

'Not today, mate.'

Scullion knew that Nick knew that everyone knew about his fall from grace. Thirty seconds after Nick had walked out of the editor-in-chief's office the whole newsfloor seemed to know his fate. Les Perger had made an example of Nick – but an example of what, nobody was quite sure.

'Still subbing?'

'That's what it said the last time I looked at the roster.'

Scullion took an involuntary step backwards, as though sub-editing was a disease that might be catching. 'So . . . why are you here?'

'Mate, I'm just a witness.'

'Yeah?'

'In the Grogan trial.'

'You know Grogan?'

'A bit.'

There was a pause. Then Scullion said, 'Anything I should know about?'

Nick shrugged. The 'should' suggested a moral imperative. Reporters like Scullion took it for granted that the world owed them information. Nick had always felt the same – until today. 'Are you lot here for Grogan?' he asked.

'Hardly,' said Scullion. 'The Love Rat's on today.'

The Love Rat – Shane Dick – was one of the *Star*'s obsessions: and these days the *Star* set the agenda for most of its rivals. It was a travesty of news values but celebrity was the driver and Shane Dick had shot to fame by coming third in an early series of *Big Brother*. Since then three different women had sued him for breach of promise. Now a fourth was claiming Dick had stolen her car for the purpose of seducing her sister. On any other day a court case involving

Danny Grogan would have made at least page three but thanks to the Love Rat, Nick could see Danny's trial being relegated to a few paragraphs on page seven. Scullion knew that too. He was already looking past Nick at the arrival of the black Toyota LandCruiser known to *Star* readers as the 'Rat Wagon' while Danny Grogan – in dark suit, dark glasses and Chicago Bears baseball cap – trudged up the stairs unnoticed.

Danny's name was second on the list for Court 1, behind a man named Parish on a break-and-enter charge. Shane Dick was listed first in Court 2. The reporters would be hoping that Parish's solicitor kept Court 1 tied up long enough for them to watch the Love Rat get his comeuppance before hotfooting it down the corridor to catch Danny Grogan in the dock. Otherwise they'd have to draw straws or it would be left to one of the agency reporters to cover Grogan.

After studying the court lists Nick went outside for a cigarette. Roy Bellamy had arrived and was standing at the bottom of the steps with a man Nick recognised from his time on police rounds as Albert Merriman QC.

As well as reputedly being Sydney's most expensive Queen's Counsel, Albert Merriman was a staple of the weekend colour magazines. He'd made his name in the 1970s defending a Kings Cross nightclub owner, Joe Steffano, from the attentions of the vice squad. One October night in 1988 Steffano was shot dead outside a Randwick laundromat by a Kings Cross detective. In the long-running trial Merriman appeared for the detective. Nick could still remember the grin on the detective's face as he and Merriman stood outside the Supreme Court, surrounded by jostling newspaper reporters and TV crews.

As the two lawyers crossed the chequerboard terrace at the top of the stairs, Merriman stopped for a moment and cast a knowing look at Nick. If the glance was meant to be reassuring, it had the opposite effect. Nick knew what to say but that didn't mean that when the time came he would be able to say it – or at least say it convincingly.

He watched the two walk inside. Danny was standing beside the vending machine. When he saw Bellamy and Merriman coming towards him he turned and walked away.

By Nick's watch it was a couple of minutes after ten. The doors had been opened. Furtive defendants and confused relatives stood up and looked at each other as if this might be the last time they would ever meet. He'd expected Danny's parents – or at least his mother – to be here but they were nowhere to be seen.

Nick finished his cigarette and tossed the butt over the balustrade and immediately lit another. He'd brought his Simenon novel to read, thinking it would help him relax. He took the book out now but couldn't concentrate. He found himself reading the same two lines over and over again: 'For a moment, it seemed that Van Damme was about to recover his self-assurance and cheerfulness, even accept the invitation to dinner . . .'

He couldn't even remember who Van Damme was, let alone who had invited him to dinner. What did it matter who Van Damme was, when in half an hour he was going to stand up, swear to tell the truth and nothing but the truth, then lie his head off to keep himself and Danny Grogan out of prison.

He stared at the sentence again. 'For a moment, it seemed that Van Damme was about to recover his self-assurance and cheerfulness, even accept the invitation to dinner . . .'

In the corner of the entrance lobby Roy Bellamy was pushing coins into the vending machine while Merriman swapped jokes with a court official. Nick couldn't see Danny; Danny wasn't there.

A sign on the wall pointed to the gents toilet. Nick walked down the corridor. As he opened the door he heard one of the toilets flush. He waited for the door to swing shut behind him. Then he said, 'Danny – are you in here?'

There was no answer. Nick bent down, as he'd seen a dozen cops do in a dozen TV shows, and walked slowly along the cubicles. In the gap beneath one door he saw a shoe. A sock was lying nearby.

'Danny,' he said, 'is that you?'

A moment later the toilet flushed. The cubicle door opened. Danny stood there, looking straight through him. His eyes were glassy.

Nick waited for several seconds before speaking. 'Did you just hit up?'

Danny didn't reply.

'Are you mad? This is a criminal court. The lobby is crawling with police.'

He grabbed Danny's arm and turned it over. Danny didn't offer any resistance. The arm was covered with bruises but Nick couldn't see anything that looked like a fresh puncture. He glanced at Danny's left shoe. The lace was undone and there was no sock on his foot. He must have injected between his toes.

'What the hell were you thinking of?'

Danny slowly focused his gaze. 'What's it to you?'

'I'm risking—' Nick lowered his voice to a fierce whisper. 'I'm risking my job to keep you out of jail.'

'I'll be fine . . . I can handle it.'

Nick remembered how Danny had looked at the club. 'When did this start?'

'Does it matter?'

'It matters to me. I'd like to know who the fuck I'm sticking my neck out for.'

Danny pushed past him to the washbasins and turned on a tap and stared for a few seconds at the water gushing down the plughole.

'I thought you'd be able to tell me that.'

Nick was still trying to work out what those words meant when he noticed a shadow behind the frosted glass. The door opened. Roy Bellamy stood there and said, 'Get out of here, Daniel.'

It was a long time since Nick had set foot inside Court 1, but little had changed except the dock, which was now surrounded by perspex walls to deter remand prisoners from impulsive escape attempts. The leather cushions on the public benches looked exactly the same as the ones he'd sat on as a cadet journalist.

As he walked through the public gallery Nick glanced at Danny, who held his gaze for a few seconds before turning away. He looked haggard, fearful. Something had gone from him, some quality of self-belief. Nick had seen other visibly drug-affected prisoners in court but not many who had shot up while waiting to be called. No doubt Albert Merriman would have explained by now that his client was on 'medication' and had dragged himself out of bed to be there.

The barrister adjusted his tobacco-stained wig and stood up. He stared for a long time at Nick without speaking. In the days and months and years to come Nick would often reflect on that gaze, wondering what it signified. While asking Nick to state his full name and address, the barrister smiled, but there was no warmth in it. 'Where were you,' he asked, 'on the night of New Year's Eve?'

'I was out. Celebrating.'

'Alone, or with friends?'

'Alone.'

'Where did you go?'

'I spent a couple of hours in the Judgment Bar.'

'This would be the Judgment Bar on Taylor Square?'

'Yes.'

'Obviously you were seen there?'

'I dare say the barman would remember me.'

'But you weren't drinking with anyone in particular?'

'No.'

'How much would you say you drank?'

'A couple of schooners. Three maybe. Light beer.'

'Not enough to be intoxicated?'

'Absolutely not.'

'You weren't tempted to stay and see in the new year?'

'I was tempted. But I left about 9.30 p.m.'

'And ran, by chance, according to your statement, into your old friend Mr Grogan?'

'That's right.'

'Who – again, according to your statement – was attempting to get into his car, which was parked on Riley Street, Darlinghurst, close to the corner of Campbell Street.'

'Yes.'

'But on recognising you, he handed you the keys and asked – "begged", I think, is the word you used – begged you to drive him home to his apartment in Bondi Beach.'

'Yes.'

'Why did he do that?'

'Danny was pretty drunk.'

'Was Danny with anyone?'

'No. Not when I saw him.'

'So he was alone in the car?'

'Unless he had someone in the boot.'

Merriman smiled indulgently. 'Did he intimate to you that he had anyone in the boot?'

'No.'

'It didn't occur to you that it might be simpler just to put him in a taxi?'

'On New Year's Eve? He would have been waiting until daylight.'

Albert Merriman obliged with a sardonic laugh while the police prosecutor shuffled some papers on her desk.

If the ritual of adversarial cross-examination hadn't been familiar to Nick from his two years as a court reporter, it would have been familiar from the countless American crime shows and made-for-TV movies he'd watched. In fact, as Nick stood there in the witness box he couldn't help feeling this *was* a made-for-TV movie, that he'd stumbled by accident onto

56

the set of a second-rate courtroom thriller. Wandering around a photogenic city like Sydney, you sometimes found yourself surrounded by location vans and catering trailers, watching a pair of actors you dimly recognised going through the motions under a thicket of lighting umbrellas. And yet, from where he stood, the role of Nick Carmody felt ambiguous. Was he the hero, or just a subsidiary character – a cameo? Was he playing the part of the faithful friend or the duplicitous accomplice?

The police prosecutor sipped a glass of water before resuming. 'So you agreed to drive him to Bondi yourself?'

'Yes.'

'But you didn't actually get that far.'

'No. Danny changed his mind. He decided he wanted to go back to the club after all.'

'Did he offer any reason for this change of heart?'

Nick helped himself to a drink of water. He'd spent long enough in Australian courts to know that what made an alibi plausible wasn't actual fact – actual fact was often absurdly implausible – but authenticity. The illusion of truth, based on the accumulation of vivid but more or less irrelevant details, was often more compelling than truth itself. 'Danny realised he'd left his phone behind,' he said. 'I saw him turning out his pockets. He took his seatbelt off. I remember him yelling at me to pull over. I thought he was going to throw up.'

'But you didn't pull over?'

'We were in the middle of Moore Park Road,' Nick said. 'There wasn't anywhere to pull over.'

'Not only did you not pull over. You put your foot down. Is that correct?'

Nick had rehearsed his evidence so many times in the days

before Danny's trial that he'd almost convinced himself it was true rather than a product of Roy Bellamy's devious imagination. And yet listening to Merriman lead him through the story, and listening to his own obedient replies reminded Nick that this was all a charade.

'Mr Carmody?' Merriman was frowning.

'Yes? I'm sorry.'

'Would you like me to repeat the question?'

'Yes . . . No . . . That's right. I put my foot down. I think I just wanted to get out of there.'

'So you don't deny speeding?'

'No,' said Nick. 'I knew I'd broken the limit.'

Merriman nodded portentously. 'So you turned the car round as soon as you were able?'

'In a side street.'

'Then what?'

'Danny had sobered up a bit. He was asking me to take him back to the club. There was some kind of party on. He told me I should come along.'

'And what was your response?'

'To be honest—' The phrase almost stuck in his throat. 'To be honest, I would just as soon have gone home. But I let him talk me into it.'

'So you drove back to the club?'

'No. I knew there were police on Taylor Square. I'd seen them from the Judgment Bar. I didn't want to risk being breathalysed. I dropped Danny off and went to find somewhere to park the car.'

Merriman ostentatiously picked up a copy of Nick's original statement. 'In Fitzroy Place?'

'That's right. It was miles away but I didn't think I'd find anywhere closer.'

'After parking Mr Grogan's car, you joined him at the club?'

'Briefly.'

'Presumably you still had his car keys in your possession?'

'I handed them to someone behind the bar.'

'And you didn't speak to Mr Grogan while you were there?'

'I spoke to him but I doubt he'd remember.'

Merriman laid Nick's statement on the desk in front of him and took out his handkerchief. 'Mr Carmody,' he said at last, 'have you been in trouble with the police before?'

'No.'

'In your account of the events of New Year's Eve is there anything you have forgotten to tell the court?'

'No.'

'Is there anything you wish to add?'

'No.'

Merriman nodded approvingly and said, 'Nothing further.'

The police prosecutor's name was Holloway. She looked about Nick's age. She had high cheekbones and slightly crossed eyes and there was something about the way she had watched Nick giving his evidence that made him think she thought he was lying. As she got to her feet Nick could feel his palms sweating. 'Will you tell the court, please, about your relationship with Mr Grogan.'

'We've known each other since we were at school.'

'The two of you are friends?'

'Yes.'

'Close friends?'

'It depends what you mean by "close".'

'If one of you was in trouble the other would want to help?'

Nick shrugged. 'Probably.'

'Probably,' Senior Constable Holloway said, looking suddenly interested. 'What exactly do you mean by that?'

'I mean it would depend what sort of help was required.'

'Let's say perjuring yourself to save Mr Grogan from a conviction that might send him to jail.'

'Objection,' Merriman said wearily, as if it was almost beneath his dignity to point out the absurdity of the point.

The magistrate – a small, prim-looking woman in her fifties – looked up. 'You'll need to do better than that, Senior Constable Holloway.'

The prosecutor stared at Nick. 'Tell the court, please, how you came to hear that your friend Mr Grogan had been arrested.'

'I was at work. I saw it on a press release.'

'You're a former crime reporter with the *Daily Star*. Is that correct?'

Nick nodded.

'Yes or no, please.'

'Yes.'

'You know something about how the media work?'

'A bit.'

'In any case, you knew about Mr Grogan's arrest long before the readers of the *Daily Star*?'

'Yes.'

'Early enough, I'd suggest, for you to start thinking about ways to help him?'

'It didn't require much thought. I knew I was the one driving Danny's car when it went through the speed camera.'

'Do you always drive that fast?'

'If I did, I wouldn't be here.'

Holloway picked up a black and white photograph and showed it to Nick. It had been taken by the speed camera in Moore Park Road. Bellamy had shown him a copy of the same photograph, though it wasn't as clear as the original. The car was Danny's. Two figures were just about visible but it was impossible to identify them, or even to say with any confidence whether they were male or female. Of course Nick knew this already. His entire statement depended on it.

The prosecutor showed Nick the photograph. 'Do you recognise this vehicle?'

'It's Danny Grogan's Audi.'

'Can you tell me who is driving it?'

Nick looked at the time printed on the photograph. 'It would have to be me.'

'Do you recognise yourself in the driver's seat?'

'No. But at the time the picture was taken, I was the driver.'

'Are you sure?'

'Quite sure.'

'From the picture it could be anyone, wouldn't you agree?'

'I suppose so.'

'It could even be Mr Grogan?'

'It could be.' Nick paused. 'But it's not.'

Senior Constable Holloway took back the photograph.

'You were aware, of course, when you agreed to drive Mr Grogan's car, that he had a history of serious motoring offences?'

'I knew Danny had been in trouble before.'

'And yet it didn't stop you from using his vehicle to break the law?'

'I didn't set out to break the law.'

'And yet—' She flicked through the contents of a cardboard folder, 'you've never had a single demerit point before now.'

'I'm used to driving a ten-year old Camry,' Nick answered. 'I got carried away.'

The door opened. He saw Danny's mother creep into the courtroom and take her place on the wooden bench closest to the dock. She didn't remove her sunglasses. It was as if she couldn't bear to be recognised, or to recognise herself.

'I put it to you,' Holloway continued, 'that the story you have just told the court is a fabrication contrived solely for the purpose of keeping your friend out of prison.'

'No,' said Nick. 'It's not.'

'I put it to you that you only came forward because the defendant's parents pleaded with you to save their son.'

'It was my decision,' said Nick. 'Nobody forced me.'

'Do you consider yourself an intelligent man, Mr Carmody?'

Intelligent. The question surprised him. He'd won a scholarship to St Dominic's. He'd fought his way over the obstacle course that weeded out 95 percent of applicants to the *Star*'s trainee program. And he'd spent the past seven years sleeping with a lawyer. Of course he considered himself intelligent. Intelligent enough to know when he was being goaded. Intelligent enough not to take the bait. He looked across at Danny, struggling to stay awake, and answered, 'Not particularly.'

'But you're not stupid?'

'I don't think so.'

'How much did Mr Grogan offer you to lie for his son?'

Nick glanced again at Danny, who looked away, as though

62

afraid to meet his gaze. And suddenly Nick had the feeling that something else was going on here, something he knew nothing about – a conspiracy he was involved in but somehow not party to. He looked at Merriman. What did the barrister know? His face gave nothing away. He was an actor, like all barristers – but did he know what part he was playing?

'Nothing,' said Nick.

'You mean he asked you to do it for nothing?'

'I mean he didn't ask me to lie for his son.'

'You and Danny Grogan were classmates. You felt you owed it to him.'

'I'm not doing this for Danny. I'm doing it for myself.'

The prosecutor stared at him for a few seconds, as though asking him to save himself. 'No further questions,' she said, and sat down.

As he stepped down from the witness stand he noticed a half-smile on Bellamy's face. What did it signify? Approval? Gratitude? Or just relief? It wasn't the sort of job any journalist should feel proud of having done, and yet he had done it, and got away with it. Nick felt something he hadn't felt before: the self-satisfaction of the successful liar. He walked out of the court and down the sandstone steps to the brick courtyard where he'd often sat as a reporter. It was here that Detective Inspector Malcolm 'Doggo' Raffles, who dealt heroin, wholesale and retail, from the children's playground opposite Redfern police station, took a swing at him for asking whether his kids would be visiting him in jail. In the shade of a plane tree a flock of pigeons was fighting over a bag of hot chips. Nick lit a cigarette and stood for a while watching the ludicrous struttings and stalkings and head-buttings. In a week or so he would be formally notified of the speeding offence to which he had already pleaded guilty and given fourteen days to pay the fine. And that, he hoped, would be the end of it.

A letter was waiting for him at home. Most of his mail was automatically redirected from the flat in Elizabeth Bay but this had been sent direct to the house in Abercrombie Street. Inside the plain white envelope was a machine-signed cheque for $8,607.45 drawn on a firm named Vaucluse Investments, made out to cash. Nick looked up the company name in the phone directory, not expecting to find it.

Over the next few weeks he would receive other cheques and look up other company names – Pacific Holdings, Consolidated Machines, Southern Cross Traders – not expecting to find them either. Experience had taught him that the Sydney phone directory wasn't the place to look for companies like these. He would have more luck searching in the Cook Islands or Costa Rica or the British Virgin Islands – tax-friendly domiciles favoured by multinational corporations and drug dealers alike. The transaction felt soiled and secretive but what had he expected – a personal cheque, presented by Harry Grogan on the steps of the Australian Stock Exchange?

Sally had been drafted to work on the State Budget. She was going to spend all day in the lock-up, attempting to make sense of the Budget papers while they were still under embargo. Jess had a runny nose, which saved her mum from having to look for excuses to keep her out of pre-school. Since Nick wasn't due at work until five, he offered to take her shopping in the city. Jess didn't like buses so they caught a train and got out at St James station, across the road from David Jones.

'I want to look at the fountain,' Jess said as they reached the middle of the pedestrian crossing.

The green pedestrian light had changed to a flashing red.

'It's too late,' said Nick. 'We'll cross the road and then come back.'

'No, it's not,' said Jess, squirming out of his grasp.

Nick just had time to snatch her up in his arms and sprint to the pavement before four lanes of traffic swept over the crossing.

'See,' said Jess. 'I was right.'

Nick's heart was racing. 'Don't do that again, Jess. You could have got us both killed.'

'Do what?' she asked.

'Slip my hand when we're crossing a busy road.'

'I didn't.'

'All right, you didn't. But don't do it again.'

Although it was clear as they walked up the path towards the Archibald Fountain that the fountain wasn't working today – and was in fact surrounded by scaffolding – Jess insisted on going all the way. 'It's not working,' she said.

'No,' said Nick. 'They must have turned it off.'

'Why?'

'I don't know. Maybe the fountain needs cleaning.'

'But it's full of water. It's already clean.'

'Maybe they've been collecting the coins.'

'Why?'

'If they didn't collect the coins from time to time then somebody would steal them.'

Jess leant over the polished wall of the fountain. 'Mummy let me throw a coin.' She frowned. 'And now it's gone.'

'Here,' said Nick, pulling a handful of coins out of his pocket. 'You can throw a couple of these.'

'Can I throw them all – please?'

'I think that's too many, Jess.'

'*Pleeease*?'

Nick shrugged and watched while Jess picked the coins out of his palm and flung them one by one into the fountain.

As they walked back through the park Nick felt a hand on his shoulder. A weedy-looking man in a white shirt and tie and grey polyester trousers was smiling at him. At first Nick took him for a Jehovah's Witness. He glanced around, looking for a companion: Jehovah's Witnesses always hunted in pairs. The man said, 'Excuse me.'

Thanks to Jess, all Nick's loose change was lying at the bottom of the Archibald Fountain. He didn't feel like giving the stranger his last twenty-dollar note. 'I'm sorry, mate,' he said. 'We're in a bit of a hurry.'

The man was pulling a clipboard out of his briefcase. He smiled at Jess. 'It won't take long. Just a few questions. If you could just spare five minutes.'

'I'm afraid we're late already.'

'No, we're not,' said Jess.

'All right, all right,' Nick said. 'Five minutes.'

The man pointed to an empty seat. 'There's a bench if you want to sit down.'

'Standing's fine.'

'My name is Robert.' The man pointed to the plastic badge on his shirt pocket. 'First of all I need to ask, are you the person primarily responsible for household cleaning chores?'

Nick knew he could have ended the interview there and then, or let Jess do it for him. But Jess was preoccupied with watching two men lugging metre-high chess pieces around an open-air board. Nick heard himself answer, 'Yes.'

With an audible sigh of relief, Robert turned the page. 'When cleaning the bath, do you prefer to use (a) liquid scourer or (b) a powdered product or (c) whatever is available?'

To Nick's shame it struck him that he had never used either, that somehow in all the years he and Carolyn had lived together, the bath had always been clean without his ever having cleaned it, or thought about cleaning it, or considered who might have cleaned it. He'd vacuumed the carpet, and he'd pulled on rubber gloves and unblocked the u-bend under the kitchen sink, but he'd never cleaned the bath. 'Always a liquid scourer,' he said.

'Good,' said Robert, although Nick couldn't tell whether it referred to the answer or simply the fact of his having answered. 'Next question. In choosing a liquid scourer, is your selection determined by (a) brand or (b) price or (c) personal recommendation by friends or family?'

To his knowledge Nick had never had a conversation with friends or family or – until now – anyone else about liquid scourers. 'Definitely brand,' he answered.

The questions went on and on, and Nick derived an odd kind of satisfaction from giving false answers. It didn't take long for him to realise that Robert's survey had been commissioned by Unilever, or one of its multinational rivals, and that Robert felt an obligation to report the sort of answers that

Unilever would want to hear. His thin mouth rose and fell according to the boxes he ticked. Most of the time it was obvious which response Robert was hoping for, and Nick was happy to deliver it. In the beginning he felt he was doing Robert a favour but gradually it dawned on Nick that he wasn't doing this for Robert. To Robert it was a job, but to him it was something else – an intellectual exercise, no, a creative exercise, a way of being himself and somehow not himself at the same time. He found it strangely exciting.

After answering all the questions Nick had to supply his first name, age, marital status and approximate income. Robert reached into his briefcase and took out a sachet of blue liquid with a sticker that said 'Not for sale – promotional use only'.

'What's this?'

'You add it to your wash. When your clothes come out they're as soft as new.'

'So it's a fabric softener?'

'Yes.'

As the market researcher trudged away in search of another victim Jess looked at Nick and said, 'You don't clean the bath. And your name's not Duncan.'

'I don't think the man was really interested in my name.'

'Then why did he ask you what it was?'

Nick put the fabric softener in his pocket. 'He needed a name, Jess, to show he wasn't making it up. I don't think he cared what name it was. I could have told him I was Bob the Builder.'

'What if he didn't believe you?' She studied him from beneath her blonde fringe. 'You should have told him your real name.'

'I was playing a bit of a game, Jess. That's all.'

'Was the man playing one too?'

Experience had taught Nick that the best way of ending an awkward conversation with Jess was to pick her up and put her on his shoulders. He picked her up and put her on his shoulders. 'Now then,' he said, 'what shall we do now?'

'Nick.'

The familiar voice came from the driver's window of a white Commodore parked in a narrow laneway near Central Station, within sight of the squat red-brick building that housed the *Daily Star*.

'Danny.'

The Commodore was parked in a space marked 'Loading Zone' outside one of the scruffy rag trade outlets that dotted the streets and lanes around the *Star*. A hand-painted sign in the shop window said 'Trade Only'.

'Can we talk?'

Nick approached the car from the driver's side, ignoring the invitation to get in. He could tell straight away that this wasn't the same Danny he'd seen in court. He looked up and down the lane. 'What do you want, Danny?'

'I should have called you. To say thanks, I mean. For getting me off the hook. I owe you, Nick. I won't forget it.'

Nick leant against the roof of the Commodore. He noticed a yellow sticker on the rear windscreen that said 'Harbourside Rentals' and wondered why Danny was driving a rented car. Maybe the insurance money hadn't come through yet. 'I'm surprised you remember any of it,' he said. 'You could hardly stay awake.'

'It wasn't my idea, Nick.'

'Don't tell me. Your father made you do it.'

'He's a hard man to refuse, Nick. He said it was the only way. I believed him.'

Nick didn't say anything. He didn't need Danny to tell him how hard it was to refuse Harry Grogan.

'Please get in, Nick. We need to talk.'

'About what, exactly?'

'Just get in. Please.'

Nick hesitated. 'Five minutes,' he said. 'That's all.'

Danny waited for him to shut the door. 'There's something you need to know.'

'There's a lot I need to know. But I don't think you can tell me, Danny.' He looked at Danny's hands gripping the steering wheel. The nails were bitten down to the quick and the skin on the inside of his wrists looked raw from rubbing. It was as if his hands belonged to someone else – as if he didn't trust himself to control them if they weren't clamped to the wheel.

'I'm clean,' said Danny. 'If that's what you're wondering.'

'Save your breath. It's none of my business.'

'Don't be like that, Nick.'

'Sorry. But I just can't think of anything you could tell me right now that I'd feel better about knowing.'

'It wasn't me who drove the car that night.'

'Yeah,' Nick answered sarcastically. 'I think I remember reading something about that.'

'It was Sophie, Nick. Sophie was behind the wheel. She wanted to score. I was already off my face. She knew this dealer . . . She's only fourteen, Nick. Do I have to spell it out?'

'You're fucking a fourteen year old?'

'I didn't know she was fourteen. She told me she was eighteen. I believed her.'

'Let me get this straight. You're telling me I lied to save your fourteen-year-old girlfriend.'

'She's not my girlfriend. I'd never seen her before that evening. I haven't seen her since. You've got to understand, Nick . . . I couldn't take the risk. It would have been statutory rape. We had to keep Sophie out of it. You're a journalist. You must understand that?'

Risk. The word detonated dully in Nick's head. Danny Grogan and his father knew all about risk. Nick had always thought of risk as something intangible, a statistical concept. But risk could be traded, just like gold or wheat or palm oil. Nick was the owner of one hundred thousand dollars worth of risk. The cheques were sitting – uncashed – in his wallet. And it turned out that he hadn't lied for Danny at all, but for some child junkie.

'Believe me. If I could have done this some other way—'

Nick cut in suddenly. 'Why did you torch the car?'

'What?'

'You went back and set light to the car. Or someone did. What was that supposed to achieve?'

'It was insured,' Danny answered lamely.

'I don't care whether it was insured. Whose idea was it to burn it?'

Danny waited a few seconds before answering. His hands were still gripping the steering wheel. 'Hers . . . I think.'

'You think?'

'Hers.'

Nick studied his expression. What did he remember about that night? It would have been a couple of days before anyone at the Roads and Transport Authority even glanced at the photographs from the speed camera. In any case, what sort of person burnt a seventy-thousand-dollar car to avoid a speeding ticket? Nick remembered the damage to the wing panel and passenger door. There was something Danny wasn't telling him, perhaps because Danny didn't know, perhaps because he knew but couldn't say.

'Why are you telling me this?' asked Nick.

Danny looked straight ahead without speaking.

'Am I supposed to be grateful? Because somehow I don't feel grateful. I feel used.'

They sat there in silence while the late afternoon traffic careened down the steep hill towards Central Station. Nick knew he was being hypocritical. He was behaving as though taking the blame for Danny had been an act of generosity when the truth was he'd been well paid for giving Danny his alibi. If it turned out that Danny wasn't the only beneficiary, did that change anything? Did a liar have any right to protest about being lied to?

Danny reached inside his jacket and pulled out a wad of fifty-dollar notes.

'What are you doing?' asked Nick.

'The fine,' Danny said. 'Six hundred dollars, wasn't it?'

Suddenly Nick felt ashamed. Maybe Danny didn't know that he'd done this for money. Maybe Danny actually believed he'd acted out of friendship. Nick let him push the six hundred dollars into his pocket.

'No need,' he murmured, 'but thanks.'

'I guess my old man would have coughed up,' said Danny, 'but I'd rather do it myself.'

Nick had his hand on the door handle. 'I've got to go, Danny . . . I've got work to do.'

'Yeah . . . me too.'

As Nick walked up the lane Danny called out, 'You should drop by the club one night . . . have something to eat.'

Nick didn't look back.

Flashing his staff card at the electronic scanner, Nick passed through the short glass tunnel designed – according to the security briefing that followed its installation – to trap any would-be terrorist or assassin in an air-tight, bullet-proof chamber, where they could be safely observed until the arrival of the police. Its more usual function, of course, was to trap employees attempting to enter the building with a damaged or expired pass or one that belonged to a colleague; all common enough ploys that had gone unpunished in the era of human security guards.

Nick entered the lift and pushed the button for the third floor: home of the canteen, the cuttings library and the well-equipped but rarely visited staff gymnasium.

The cuttings library occupied a corner of what had been the compositors' room, until the compositors were made redundant and the presses were moved out. When Nick had started as a copy boy the library had a staff of half a dozen and clipped every newspaper in Sydney as well as the national dailies, the Melbourne *Age*, the *Bulletin* and a couple of Fleet Street papers.

As well as the *Star*'s own archives, there were cuttings from the *Herald*, the *Sun* and the *Mirror* going back as far as the Second World War and even beyond. On his breaks from fetching pictures, making coffee and buying cigarettes, Nick used to enjoy browsing among the files of brittle brown newsprint.

Over the years successive management regimes had retrenched staff and uprooted files for so-called 'long-term storage' at a warehouse in the western suburbs. In the meantime every story that went into the *Star* was now automatically archived by the huge computer that whirred and muttered away in its own air-conditioned glass pod on the eighth floor. The few remaining library staff were supposed to be working backwards, systematically transferring newsprint files to computer discs, but the truth was they didn't have time to do it. So, for the *Daily Star*, recorded history now began somewhere in the early 1990s. Before that there were only fragments.

After chatting briefly with one of the female librarians, Nick sat down at an empty computer terminal. Jerry Whistler would be at the afternoon news conference until 4.30 p.m. and none of the other subs would care if Nick was a few minutes late.

At the log-in prompt he was about to type in his own name and password when he changed his mind and typed in SUB1 – a generic user-name for casual subeditors and anyone else who'd forgotten their password.

It puzzled him that nobody had reported the destruction of Danny's Audi. During the court hearing it had been mentioned only once. The police seemed willing to believe that whoever had ripped out the stereo had also incinerated the car. There was no evidence to suggest that the destruction of Danny's Audi was anything other than a macabre coincidence.

He typed the name 'Danny Grogan' into the search box, together with the words 'Audi' and 'burnt'. There was no shortage of would-be satirists around town ready and willing to hammer out a few hundred words of laborious whimsy at Danny Grogan's expense – Jerry Whistler for one. The computer hummed for a few seconds before displaying the message: NO ARTICLE MATCHED YOUR SEARCH CRITERIA. PLEASE MODIFY SEARCH AND TRY AGAIN.

Nick deleted the word 'burnt' and tried again. This time the search produced four results. The first was a picture story from page three of the Sunday *Star*, with a photograph of Danny standing alongside his 'brand new toy – a gleaming German speed machine with the cheeky numberplate CR1PT'. The second, also from the Sunday *Star*, showed Danny and his girlfriend of the moment, posing in Formula One suits at Eastern Creek International Raceway before a charity event in which Danny finished third. The other two stories were both from the *Daily Star*: a front-page news report the morning after Danny was arrested for drink-driving outside the Bat and Ball Hotel, and a report of the trial at Waverley Local Court, where Danny escaped with a suspended sentence.

It was nearly 4.30 p.m. Nick logged off the computer and walked out of the library and down the long windowless corridor to the lift. The search hadn't told him much – except, perhaps, that if the police really had found anything suspicious in Danny Grogan's car, they were keeping it to themselves.

He got out on the editorial floor and headed straight for the male toilets. Moments later he found himself, rather awkwardly, standing next to the editor-in-chief, Les Perger.

Staring resolutely at the white ceramic tiles, Nick mumbled, 'Hello, Les.'

'Nick,' Perger replied in a tone that was, as usual, devoid of any semblance of warmth or even courtesy, even though it was Perger himself who had hired him.

75

They stood shoulder-to-shoulder as the editor-in-chief wrestled with his flies.

'See the paper this morning?' Perger asked. 'The gambling yarn was all over the radio news.'

'So I heard,' said Nick.

The 'gambling yarn' was the sort of story that defined the *Star* under Les Perger. A mother playing the pokies at her local RSL had left her two children locked in the car. The carpark attendant found the children, smashed a window to let them out and then, charitably, phoned the *Star*. Nick hadn't needed to be present at the midday news conference to recognise Les Perger's hand in the decision to put the children back in the car for a picture, which showed two little faces gazing shyly through the broken glass under the headline, HOW COULD SHE?

'Tracey did a nice job,' said Perger.

'Very nice.'

'She's a smart girl.'

Nick zipped up and waited for Perger to add the ironic rider he felt certain was coming. For a man of such volatile temper, with a long record of tearing doors off their hinges, Perger could be disarmingly patient. You never knew whether it was better to admit and apologise for a mistake or to brazen it out in the hope that Perger had more important things to worry about.

The naming and shaming of dangerous drivers had been one of Les Perger's first innovations as editor-in-chief of the *Star*. Gone was the back-page picture of the dog of the week, banished to some rarely visited space among the weather details; in its place was a mug shot, the less flattering the better, of a recently convicted dangerous driver, together with the numberplate of the offending vehicle. Mocked – and then copied – by the broadsheet *Herald*, this was vigilante journalism and Les Perger was its acknowledged master. For some reason Nick had forgotten all about Perger's dangerous driver obsession when agreeing to provide Danny Grogan with an alibi.

Perger followed him to the row of basins and squirted pink soap into the palm of his hand.

'Listen, Les,' said Nick. 'I'm sorry about the Grogan thing.'

'What Grogan thing is that?'

'I never thought it would end up in court.'

Perger stood there lathering his huge hands. 'You thought you might sort it out over a few beers, did you, Nick?'

'The police wouldn't accept my statement. There wasn't a lot I could do about it.'

'They reckoned old man Grogan put you up to it – is that the story?'

'Something like that.'

'And did he, Nick? Did the old crook put you up to it?'

Nick was startled by the question, and by Perger's casual use of the word 'crook'. Of course Harry Grogan's ruthlessness, his bullying, his duplicity, were qualities known to anyone who had ever glanced at the business pages of a major newspaper. Grogan had demonstrated them all during his celebrated appearance before a public inquiry into price-fixing in the building industry. His fifteen-minute cameo, shoulders hunched over the table as if at any moment he might lean forwards and bite the microphone in half, had been endlessly replayed on television. At least two promising legal careers had died in that wood-panelled room, as Grogan hectored and ridiculed his questioners, wagging his finger at the counsel assisting every time she attempted to bring him back to the question. But 'crook'?

Rumours abounded about Harry Grogan's involvement in the fatal amusement park fire that proved so profitable to his company, but despite the efforts of a coronial inquiry not a shred of evidence had ever been found to prove it. And there was no shortage of scuttlebutt to explain the cosy relationship between Grogan Constructions and the New South Wales Department of Public Works, but all of it was hearsay. Like every other newspaper in Sydney, the *Star* had paid out handsomely over the years in libel damages when such insinuations found their way into print. On the other hand Les Perger wasn't the sort of man to throw around a word like 'crook' without knowing something.

'Shit, no,' he said. 'I was the one driving the car.'

'Yeah? Well, that's all right then.'

Their eyes met in the mirror. There was something in Perger's lopsided smile that made it clear to Nick that everything was far from all right.

'It was an Audi TT,' said Nick. 'I just got carried away. I didn't even notice the speedo.'

Perger shook the water off his hands. 'You read this newspaper, don't you, Nick?' Rule number one at the *Daily Star* and every other newspaper in the world: the journalist who can't be bothered to read his own paper will soon be looking for another job.

'Of course, Les.'

'So you know what we think about dangerous drivers.'

Nick reached for a paper towel, but the dispenser was empty. 'Yes, Les.'

'Yes, Les,' said Perger. Nick knew what was coming next. First the moronic repetition. Then the word 'mate'. It was like a replay of the Milhench fiasco, only worse. Far worse. Then Nick was the scapegoat, sacrificed for an error of judgment Perger himself might easily have been guilty of in his youth. Even as Perger chastised him for his 'cowboy' reporting, Nick had the feeling that, secretly, he approved – that what Perger wanted for his newspaper was a staff full of cowboys. That hadn't saved Nick, of course. Bombarded with phone calls from the premier, the minister of police and the chief commissioner, and threatened with the wholesale withdrawal of government advertising, the editor-in-chief had done what he had to do and hung Nick out to dry – on the foreign subs' desk, under Jerry Whistler.

'Mate,' said Perger. 'Have you any idea how this makes us look – like fucking hypocrites.'

'If you think it's damaged my byline, I'm sorry.'

Perger glanced at the empty paper towel dispenser, then walked to the other wall and tugged on the roller towel. 'If you had a byline to damage, mate, I'd be worried.'

He didn't need to say any more, and he didn't say any more. Nick listened to him slapping his palms together as he strode away down the corridor.

The evening went slowly. Nick spent nearly an hour blending wire stories for a potential page one story about a plane crash in the Philippines. Filipino authorities were reporting two honeymooning Australians among the seventy-nine dead: if the picture editor could get photographs of the newlyweds to put side-by-side with the crash scene it would have been a shoo-in for tomorrow's splash. At 9.15 p.m., with reporters and cadets and a couple of copy girls ransacking the phone book for people with the same name as the crash victims, a report came down the Reuters wire saying the couple weren't honeymooners or even Australians but middle-aged Filipinos with family in Brisbane, transforming the story in a flash to three paragraphs on page twelve.

Having the splash was always a coup for the *Star*'s under-appreciated foreign desk, and losing it put Jerry Whistler in a foul mood. For the next hour, he and Nick didn't speak to each other. Then Jerry said, 'I'm going across the road for a beer. Are you coming?'

You could say one thing for Jerry Whistler: he'd never had a tantrum that couldn't be cured by the prospect of half an hour in the back bar of the Evening Star hotel.

'No thanks,' Nick said. 'I've got a couple of phone calls to make.'

Jerry shrugged, 'Your loss, old boy.' He was halfway to the corridor when he shouted back, 'If Reuters change their mind about those Filipinos, we'll whack it in for the second edition.'

'Sure.'

Nick was still thinking about his conversation with Les Perger. He'd made mistakes before and always come back. Perger admired initiative and Nick had always shown plenty of that. But Perger had made it sound as though his exile on the foreign desk might be more than just temporary. What if his reporting career was over? Perger was a tyrant and it was in the nature of tyrants to keep reminding you of the fact. To err was human, the editor-in-chief liked to say, but to keep erring was the preserve of the broadsheets. The *Daily Star* didn't run a 'We were wrong' column because there was no 'we'. Serious offenders were rooted out and punished, by name. Sitting there, watching Jerry

Whistler's pear-shaped body waddle across the newsroom, Nick saw his banishment stretching away for years, until he slunk at last to some pseudo-managerial job that nobody else would do – cadet training manager, for instance. Nick Carmody, cadet training manager. The thought made him shudder.

He got up and stretched his arms behind his back and walked over to talk to the night chief of staff, an Englishman named Brian Cockburn. The title night chief of staff implied ambition and enterprise although the job didn't need either. Most of the paper had been filled before the night chief of staff even sat down but now and then something happened – a fire, a police chase, somebody famous at the airport – and a reporter would have to be found to cover it. Night chief of staff was one of a handful of jobs that Jerry Whistler had his eye on.

Whether or not Brian Cockburn had worked for the Fleet Street papers he claimed to have worked for, in the capacity in which he claimed to have worked for them, was a moot point by now. Brian had long ago accepted that his career at the *Star* was going to stall at night chief of staff and seemed determined to make the best of it. From what Nick could see he spent most of his evenings sketching plots for the thriller he was going to write when he retired. He wasn't bitter and Nick liked him.

'Nick,' he said, as though surprised to see him. 'I've been looking for you.'

'I've been sitting at my desk since 4.30,' said Nick.

'Yeah,' said Cockburn. 'It was after that. Probably around nine o'clock.'

Nine o'clock was roughly when Nick had gone outside to smoke a cigarette. It had just started to rain. Huddled under the bronze awning, he'd spent a few minutes innocently –

well, semi-innocently – chatting up one of the copy girls. He frowned. 'What was?'

'Michael was looking for you.'

'Michael?'

'Flynn. Crime reporter.' Cockburn paused before adding archly, 'Your gallant successor. He had some bee in his bonnet about something. I said I'd keep an eye out for you.'

'Well here I am. Where's Flynn?'

'Heading for the lift last time I saw him.'

'So it wasn't important?'

'I suppose it can't have been.'

Nick wandered off in the direction of the fire stairs, where three members of the sports subs' desk were illegally smoking in the stairwell. Seeing him approach, they nodded and invited him to join them. One bummed a cigarette. Their cigarette hands rose and fell in unison, like a team of synchronised smokers. The one who'd bummed a cigarette – a laconic Vietnam veteran whom Nick knew only as Zippo – said, 'Flynn was looking for you.'

'So I heard,' said Nick.

As a fellow smoker in an increasingly tobacco-free workplace, Nick had almost daily conversations with Zippo and yet the only thing he knew about him was that he'd served in Vietnam – and he hadn't heard that from Zippo.

'I don't suppose he said what it was about.'

Zippo shook his crew-cut head as he exhaled. 'Didn't ask.'

Nick finished his cigarette and ground it out beneath his heel and kicked the mangled filter down the stairwell. While the others slowly climbed the stairs to the editorial floor, Nick took out his mobile phone and dialled Danny Grogan's number. He was curious to know whether Flynn had been in touch with him since the trial. There was something about Flynn he didn't trust: the fact that he spoke Mandarin, perhaps. Why would a Mandarin-speaker want to work on the *Daily Star*, whose only foreign bureaus were in London and Los Angeles? Nick waited for the ring tone but Danny's phone was either switched off or out of range.

He felt apprehensive without knowing why. The edition was a few minutes away. The last reporter had gone home for the night and subeditors were still straggling in from the Evening Star. There was no sign of Jerry Whistler. Nobody paid any attention to Nick as he walked across the newsroom to the row of steel filing cabinets along the back wall. He bent down. His heart thumped as he unlocked the drawer marked 'Carmody'. He opened the drawer and took out the envelope containing the five thousand dollars in cash given to him by Danny Grogan's father. He resisted the temptation to open the envelope and count it. Looking over his shoulder, he noticed Jerry Whistler talking to Brian Cockburn. He stuffed the envelope in his pocket and locked the drawer and walked back to his desk.

The lights were on when Nick got home. Usually it was only the dog that waited up, quivering on the doormat in the hope that, at one o'clock in the morning, Nick might change his mind about going to bed and decide instead to go for a walk around the crime-ridden streets of Chippendale. They had met in Prince Alfred Park in the early hours of a January morning and some-where in the back of its tiny greyhound brain was a belief that they had never left. Looking into its pleading eyes, Nick was touched by the animal's faith in him, its perpetual willingness to overcome and forgive disappointment. He squatted between the bicycles and stroked its bumpy skull, and the dog in turn slapped its tail against the floorboards.

The living-room door opened. Sally was standing there in her dressing gown and somehow Nick knew, by the look on her face, what she was going to say.

'Nick. Michael's here. He's been waiting for you.'

Flynn was on his feet and standing in front of the red chintz sofa with his hands, bizarrely, on his hips. What did a stance like that convey – embarrassment? Menace? Or some esoteric combination of both? Nick noticed a bottle of whisky – he'd never seen Sally drinking spirits before – and two glasses on the low table between the sofa and the battered leather armchair. No ashtray, of course, since Nick had agreed not to smoke in the house. Flynn had his hand out. He had a surprisingly firm grip. 'Nick. I know it's late . . . '

Nick glanced involuntarily at his watch, although he knew exactly what time it was. He could smell the whisky on Flynn's breath. 'Michael. What's this about?'

Flynn and Sally exchanged glances, and Nick wondered what he'd told her.

'Look,' said Sally, 'why don't I leave you guys alone?'

Flynn didn't say anything.

Nick said, 'Sorry you had to wait up, Sal.' He was going to add, 'It won't take long to sort this out' but as he opened his mouth he sensed Flynn looking at him and left the words unsaid.

On her way out Sally turned to Nick. 'There's some Scotch left if you feel like it.' She wasn't smiling and Nick wondered again what she knew.

'I'll put the dog out,' Nick said as Sally shut the door behind her.

Flynn was standing, with his hands in his pockets this time, as if he didn't know what else to do with them, although this hardly seemed to Nick like a hands-in-pockets sort of occasion. He sat down in the armchair and waited for Flynn to reclaim his place on the sofa.

'All right, Michael. Why don't you tell me what's going on?'

It was almost 1.15 a.m. He wanted to be in bed.

'I don't know you very well,' Flynn began, 'but I wanted to give you the benefit of the doubt.'

'That's good of you. But in relation to what?'

'Everyone reckons you were a bloody good reporter.'

'Are, not were. I'm not dead yet.'

'From what I heard you got a raw deal over the Milhench arrest.'

'You mean the Milhench non-arrest?'

'Yes.'

'Is that what this is about?'

'No.'

'Listen, Michael. It's late. I've been subbing wire copy all night. Could you skip the preamble and just tell me why you're here.'

'Danny Grogan.'

Nick folded his arms, then wished he hadn't. In his experience folded arms meant having something to hide. Ignoring his promise not to smoke in the house, he reached for his cigarettes. Somehow, from the moment he'd laid eyes on Flynn, he'd been bracing himself to hear those words.

'What about him?'

'He's a friend of yours, right?'

'Was. We were at school together. I don't see much of him these days.'

'But you saw him on New Year's Eve.'

'Unfortunately, yes.'

'You drove his car.'

'Yes.'

'A metallic blue Audi TT coupe.'

'Michael. I've had this conversation in front of a magistrate. It cost me six hundred dollars and four points off my licence. And in case you're wondering, Les Perger knows all about it.' He looked at his watch. 'So if that's your scoop, mate, you're running a bit behind the pack.'

Flynn ignored the patronising tone. He sat for a while watching Nick smoke. Then he said, 'What if I told you that a car just like Grogan's was involved in an accident that night?'

'Not while I was driving.'

'You're sure of that?'

'Where was this accident?'

'Randwick.' Flynn paused. 'Just a few kilometres from where you were clocked speeding.'

'Bullshit. Someone's pulling your leg, Michael.'

'Are they?'

'Who did you get this from – one of those dopey buggers in media liaison?'

'This didn't come from media liaison.'

'Who then?'

Flynn didn't answer. Nick hadn't expected him to: he wouldn't have answered himself.

'What sort of accident?'

'A hit-and-run.'

Nick vaguely recalled the *Star* reporting a hit-and-run on the night of New Year's Eve. The victim, he remembered, was a middle-aged man. There had been no mention of witnesses. The police hadn't even known what sort of car they were looking for. 'What about the rego?'

'The witness didn't catch it. So I'm told.'

So there was a witness. But a witness to what? And why had it taken so long for this witness to come forward?

'If he didn't catch—'

'She. The witness was female.'

'Fine. If she didn't catch the rego, how come she was so sure about the car?'

'Audi TT coupe,' said Flynn. 'It's the kind of car you'd remember.'

'Maybe. Maybe not.' Nick ground the butt of his cigarette into Sally's whisky tumbler. 'Listen, Michael. A bit of friendly advice. There are some bitter and twisted people in the world and quite a few of them wear blue uniforms. I wouldn't exactly describe Danny Grogan as Mr Popular down at Police Headquarters.'

'But Grogan wasn't driving his car that night,' said Flynn. 'You were – or have I got that wrong?'

Nick lit another cigarette. To deny he was the driver was to admit to perverting the course of justice. The thought suddenly occurred to him that Flynn might have spoken to Danny. Was that why Nick hadn't been able to reach him? Was Danny avoiding him?

'The victim was a dealer,' said Flynn. 'The word is, he was a sleazy customer. He was into other forms of payment.'

Nick realised he was being backed into a corner. He couldn't rely on Danny to get him out. An awful realisation dawned on him. What if it had all been a set-up? Nick thought about the incinerated car. Supposing Danny – or the girl – had hit someone. They burnt the car, hoping that would destroy the evidence. Maybe they heard about the witness, maybe they didn't. In any case they needed an alibi. The speeding ticket was just the bait they needed to draw him in. It would have been too much to expect Nick to put his hand up for a fatal hit-and-run. But a speeding ticket? For a hundred thousand dollars Nick was just stupid enough to agree to that. A hot sick feeling went through him like a wave.

'The way I heard it,' said Flynn, 'the car must have hit him twice.'

Flynn's engine wouldn't start. Nick switched off the light and stood in the hallway while the starter motor choked and snarled. Finally the engine spluttered into life. Flynn sat there revving the accelerator before driving away.

Why had he come – to warn or to threaten? Nick had stuck to his story, because he had no choice. But the story had changed. Tomorrow or the next day or the next, two detectives were going to walk through the door – or maybe they would come for him at work – and charge him with manslaughter, or worse. He could deny it but what good would that do him? It was his word now against his word in court, on oath. He was lying now or he'd been lying then.

He thought about the money: five thousand dollars and a wad of uncashed cheques. Without it, he could have argued that he'd lied for Danny out of a misguided sense of loyalty. Breaking up with Carolyn had left him vulnerable to an appeal by an old friend. He'd acted out of character. As a court reporter Nick had heard similar excuses dozens of times. Sometimes a magistrate believed them – or pretended to. Sometimes Nick even believed them himself. And yet he knew in his heart that people didn't act out of character. They acted in character. They just didn't recognise it.

He went into the kitchen and shut the door and tried ringing Danny. His phone was still switched off. He found Danny's home number in an old contact book but the phone rang out. He wasn't sure that Danny could help him but he knew that without Danny he didn't have a chance.

A floorboard creaked – or was it the balcony swaying in the wind? Nick stood at the bottom of the stairs, listening. He wondered if Sally was still awake. Could he confide in her – in anyone? The dog gave one of its agonised yawns – the yawn of an animal that knew that any moment now it was going to be put outside. Nick reached down and stroked its skull. Then he put it outside.

From the kitchen Jess called out, 'I'm feeding myself.'

'Jess is feeding herself,' said Sally. 'She wants you to have a look. Please applaud. The more applause she gets the more likely she is to do it again.'

'Good girl, Jess,' said Nick. In Sally's presence he always sounded more formal towards Jess than he intended.

'I made a mess,' Jess replied proudly, leaning over the tray of her high chair to indicate a smudge of Weetbix-coloured mush on the ancient linoleum floor.

89

'Come on,' said Nick. 'Let me see another mouthful of Weetbix.'

Jess dipped her plastic spoon into the milk.

'Milk first,' said Jess.

Sally was watching him and not moving and for a moment Nick had the disconcerting feeling that she was frightened of him. She untied and re-tied the knot in her dressing gown. 'What's going on, Nick?'

Even if he'd wanted to answer that question truthfully, he wouldn't have known how. He walked up to Sally and put an arm around her. She let him but her own arms remained by her side. 'It's nothing,' he said.

'Then why was Michael so anxious to see you?'

'He was working on a story. For some reason he wanted to run it past me.'

'At one o'clock in the morning?'

Nick didn't answer.

Sally took Jess's plastic spoon out of her mouth. 'Come on, darling,' she said. 'You mustn't stop just because Nick is here.'

'I want to watch something,' said Jess.

'No, Jess. We had an agreement. You can watch something after you've had breakfast.'

'I want to watch something now.'

'I'll feed her,' said Nick.

'You shouldn't encourage her blackmail,' said Sally.

Nick stirred the Weetbix until it was a formless paste. 'She's almost finished. Haven't you, Jess?'

'I'm almost finished,' Jess agreed.

'Has this got something to do with Danny Grogan?'

'It might have.'

Sally stared at him. 'Were you really driving the car?' She gripped his forearm for a few seconds before releasing it. 'I'm not the police, Nick. You can tell me.'

'Admitting it cost me six hundred dollars. Why would I say I was driving the car if I wasn't?'

'I don't know.'

'I don't want to talk about this, Sal. It's bad enough having to tell Flynn—' He stopped himself.

'Tell Flynn what?'

'Nothing.'

'Are you in trouble, Nick?'

'It's just a misunderstanding. I'll talk to Flynn. I'll sort it out.'

The story was on the ABC news as Nick got out of the shower. A body believed to be that of Danny Grogan, proprietor of the Crypt nightclub in Oxford Street, Darlinghurst, had been found around dawn in the stairwell of an apartment building in Bondi, not far from where he lived. The body was spotted by a man delivering newspapers. According to the news report it hadn't been formally identified but the delivery man had recognised Danny. The building was cordoned off and police were interviewing residents to discover whether Danny had visited any of the apartments. Cause of death was yet to be determined but according to an ambulance officer on the scene Danny had died of an overdose.

Nick stood there dripping on the floorboards, unable to move. He was alone in the house. Sally and Jess had gone into the city to buy shoes. Sally had seemed anxious not to be in the house with him. She had shut the door without saying goodbye. Nick tied the towel around his waist and sat down on the bed.

Poor Danny. Poor stupid wretched Danny. Nick remembered the way he'd kept rubbing his wrists in the car, like someone worrying at a stain that wouldn't go away. Danny wasn't clean. Danny would never be clean.

A semi downshifted before the traffic lights at Broadway. Nick listened to the gurgle of the diesel engine as the driver worked his way methodically through the gears. Danny's death had left him with only two options: to stick with his story or retract it and face the consequences. Only it wasn't his story. It never had been his story. It had been written for him by Roy Bellamy: all he'd had to do was learn his lines. No, the story had been Danny's all along but now Danny was dead. He was up to his neck in trouble but there was a way out if only he could find it. There was always a way out: proof of that simple truth turned up every day in the crowded columns of the *Daily Star*.

What he needed now was time. This wasn't a problem that would go away in a day or a week. Danny Grogan was dead and what happened next was up to Nick. He could wait for the police and Michael Flynn to burst through the door waving their warrants and notebooks, or he could disappear while he still had the chance. He looked at his watch. Sally and Jess would be back by eleven. He had fifty-three minutes to make up his mind.

His ten-year-old Toyota Camry was parked in Abercrombie Street, close to the corner with Cleveland Street. Nick stared at a picture of a well-dressed, middle-aged Caucasian man which someone had taped to a lamppost. The man was smiling at the person taking the picture. (Why did missing men always smile?) There was a black-and-white dog in the background. In heavy type – like a front-page headline in the *Daily Star* – were the words HAVE YOU SEEN THIS MAN? followed by a mobile phone number. In their eagerness to publicise his disappearance, the missing man's family had somehow forgotten to give his name.

Pictures like it were sent to the *Daily Star* at a rate of one or two a week – often double that in summer. Sometimes they found their way into the paper, squeezed into an uncommercial gap between display advertisements or buried among the classifieds on a Saturday. Most, however, were simply filed away in the photographic library in cardboard document boxes marked 'Missing'.

Nick studied the pixelated photograph. Had it been taken by his wife? A friend? A stranger? What could you tell from a photograph anyway? The man was smiling. Maybe he was happy then – or maybe he was just pretending for the sake of the photographer. The picture might have been years old. Lives changed but a photograph was fixed forever. Nick stared at the smiling man and wondered if he would ever be found.

Nick opened the door and watched the greyhound screw itself into the back seat. He'd intended to leave it behind but the dog seemed to know exactly what was in Nick's mind, and wouldn't let him out of its sight. Nick, too, knew that within twenty-four hours of his going, Sally would be on the phone to the South Sydney council dog catcher. If Nick vanished, the animal was going to vanish with him.

North or south? Nick's instinct was to disappear among the hordes moving up the coast to Queensland. It was like a mass internal migration, from the rust belt to the sun belt. And yet it was the south that had always appealed to him: the long pristine beaches of the south coast, the grey forests, the temperamental summers and cold winters. Jervis Bay, Lake

Conjola, Bermagui, Merimbula, Eden – he remembered visiting those places as a child, dragging his parents' old wooden caravan from camp site to camp site until it literally fell apart on a dirt road in Ben Boyd national park.

He turned the key in the ignition, put the Camry into gear and drove to the corner of Broadway, waiting for the traffic lights to change. On the passenger seat beside him was a green nylon sportsbag filled with clothes. He realised he'd left behind an almost new pair of Reebok trainers. It was too late to go back for them now.

At a Caltex service station on the Princes Highway he stopped to check the tyres and clean the windscreen and fill up with petrol. Twenty minutes later the sight of a police patrol car in his rear-view mirror tightened his knuckles around the steering wheel. Between the shock of Danny's death and the excitement of leaving he'd almost forgotten Flynn. Whatever Flynn knew – or thought he knew – he'd jumped the gun by telling Nick and had given him a precious few hours' head start. Sally would think he'd just taken the dog for a walk. It would be mid-afternoon before she began to wonder.

The ugly southern suburbs rolled away behind him. Nick found his gaze drawn to the newspaper posters outside railway stations and on the walls of newsagents' shops. Of course there was no mention of Danny. Dying in the small hours was Danny's final revenge on the *Daily Star*, ensuring it was twenty-four hours late with the news.

It was a few minutes after midday. The morning news conference would have just started. Les Perger would probably give up half tomorrow's paper to documenting the dissolute life and squalid death of Danny Grogan. Most of it would be rehashed from the files. No doubt the picture editor would stake out the mansion in Vaucluse, hoping for a photograph of the grieving mother. Ken Horswill, commercial talkback host and conscience of the *Star*, would deliver a thousand ghosted words on the wasted life of a spoilt rich boy.

Nick's name was certain to come up at the news conference. Maybe this would have been his chance to redeem himself with a heart-wrenching yarn on the Danny Grogan he knew. But how would it end – with Danny shooting up in a toilet cubicle in Central Local Court? Or sitting in a rental car while he confessed to sleeping with a fourteen-year-old junkie? No, Danny might be dead but there was still something Nick could offer him: silence.

Within a few hours Jerry Whistler would know he wasn't coming to work. Jerry would ring Sally and Sally would tell him . . . what? That Nick had disappeared and taken the dog?

His mobile started ringing. The caller ID was an extension at the *Daily Star*. Nick let it ring out. He stopped at Kiama and bought a couple of bottles of water and something to eat. He walked up the hill and stood for a few minutes among a Japanese coach party watching geysers of water erupting from the blowhole.

A green sign pointed to Seven Mile Beach. Nick had been there once with Danny and a friend of Danny's whose name he couldn't remember: three eighteen year olds and a bong flying down the Princes Highway on a Friday night in a Range Rover that Danny claimed to have 'borrowed' for the weekend. The three of them had slept on the beach and when Nick woke up cold and stiff and with his hair full of sand he noticed Danny standing in the dunes watching a humpback whale. He stayed there all morning, unable to drag himself away.

Nick turned off the highway and followed a winding road through flat woodland to the coast.

The small gravel carpark was deserted except for a white Valiant panel van. Wooden planking ran over the dunes, which had been fenced for plant regeneration. In the distance he saw a shape that looked like a person – probably the driver of the white panel van – sitting in the dunes. Nick walked down to the firm wet sand while the dog ran ahead, scampering into the waves and retreating before the tumbling surf. Then Nick turned, walking away from the figure in the dunes.

The weather was less benign than it had been that morning. The sky out to sea was a forbidding grey, with cooling towers of cloud piled up on the horizon. A blustery wind blew veils of spray off the crests of the waves. After an hour Nick turned back. The beach felt deserted, seven miles of sand with nobody's footprints but his own. As he neared the spot where he'd parked his car he looked for the figure in the dunes but whoever it was had moved or gone. He climbed the planking and stood on the dune, gazing at the grey sea, half imagining that if he stood there long enough he might catch sight of Danny's whale.

He lit a cigarette and sat in his car with the door open while the dog explored the bushes. After he'd smoked his cigarette he took a swig of bottled water and turned to look at the white panel van. A tatty net curtain had been part-drawn across the rear window. Nick wondered if someone was sleeping inside. He screwed the lid back on the bottle and switched on the car radio and sat for a while thinking.

After a few minutes he stood up and walked across the carpark. The panel van was parked facing the sea. It couldn't have been there long or else the windscreen would have been encrusted with salt spray. Slowly, he walked around it. He could see now that there was nobody inside. The tailgate wasn't properly fastened. Through the net curtain he could see a rolled-up mattress, a pair of old trainers and some boxes of supermarket groceries – as if the owner was preparing to go on a trip. Nick lifted the tailgate. The air inside the car smelt of dope. A bong was resting against the wheel arch.

Nick closed the tailgate again. He walked back to the dunes and looked up and down the beach. He couldn't see a soul. Then he returned to the panel van and opened the driver's door. The key was still in the ignition. He walked around to the other side and popped open the glove box. Inside was a black rubber-handled torch; a pouch of loose tobacco and a couple of plastic lighters; a scuffed leather wallet; some cheap sunglasses and a handful of ATM and credit card receipts.

What sort of person, Nick asked himself, left his wallet and ignition key in an unlocked car?

Twelve years on the *Star* had given him an instinct for the irrational, the unfinished, the absurd. Broadsheets like the *Herald* believed in neat endings. But the tabloids knew that stories often stopped, or faded away, or turned back on themselves, and that the most interesting followed only their own skewed logic.

Years ago someone had left a yellow briefcase full of money beneath a desk in the reading room of the State Library. In those days there were no security cameras and neither the guard at the door nor any of the librarians nor anyone who'd visited the library that day could remember seeing anyone carrying a yellow briefcase. The publicity brought out several claimants but none of them could prove the case was theirs and the money was probably still gathering interest in some obscure government account.

Over the years Nick had often thought about the vanished owner of that yellow briefcase. He thought of him now as he took the leather wallet out of the glove box and opened it.

The wallet contained seventy dollars in cash, a Westpac VISA card and ATM card, and a New South Wales driver's licence. The driver's name was Kevin Michael Chambers of Prospect Road, Canley Vale, in Sydney's western suburbs. According to his date of birth Chambers was a year and a half older than Nick.

The licence was four years old. At a careless glance the photograph bore a vague resemblance to pictures of Nick taken a few years ago, before his hair started to thin. He and Kevin Chambers had the same colour hair – a sort of dirty straw blond – and similarly oval faces, both clean-shaven. The likeness was subliminal rather than overwhelming but in a strange way that made it all the more plausible. After all, Nick had official photographs of himself that didn't look anything like him: the photograph in his own passport, for example. And a careless glance was all that most people gave to the small photographs pushed across the counter for verification.

He put the licence back in the leather wallet and lit a cigarette. What if he were to swap vehicles? A couple of times on the highway north of Kiama he'd had the sensation of being followed. But it was never more than a sensation and when he'd pulled over and waited for the traffic to pass he'd realised he was just imagining it. Nevertheless, it wouldn't be long before the police started looking for his red Camry. The Camry was worth at least twice what anyone would give Chambers for his beaten-up panel van.

It was impulse rather than calculation. If he'd thought about it for another five minutes, another two minutes, another two seconds, perhaps he would have decided against it. Impulse had warned him against taking Harry Grogan's money and he'd ignored it – and found himself set up for a fatal hit-and-run. Maybe it was time to act on impulse.

He opened the tailgate and transferred a couple of boxes to the boot of his Camry. As he walked back with the third the bottom collapsed. Tins of tuna and baked beans and bags of rice and dried pasta tumbled out. An exploding jar splattered the legs of his jeans with pasta sauce. Jagged shards of glass lay all over the gravel. Nick grabbed the shoes and the bong and the rolled-up mattress from the back of the panel van and slammed the tailgate on a carton of fruit and vegetables. Then he took two hundred dollars out of his wallet and stuffed it in the Camry's glove box.

He sat behind the steering wheel of the white panel van and turned the key in the ignition. The engine started straight away. Nick watched the fuel gauge needle creep towards full. A butt in the ashtray reminded him that he'd run out of cigarettes. Leaving the engine running, he walked across the gravel and fetched the bag containing his clothes. The dog seemed to sense what was happening. It trotted after him and, when Nick opened the tailgate, the animal leapt in.

Nick spent a minute searching for gears on the unfamiliar shift. He revved the four-litre V8, then put the stick into gear and reversed out of the carpark.

A vehicle like this, Nick thought, was liable to be recognised, so he by-passed the few shabby motels in Shoalhaven Heads and headed instead for Ulladulla, searching his mirror all the way.

Glancing at the ashtray reminded him that he was dying for a cigarette. He was dying for the cigarette he'd been dying for since he left Seven Mile Beach. It was just after 7 p.m. He stopped at a service station on the outskirts of Nowra and bought a packet of Winfields and a bottle of Coca-Cola and a shapeless, formless pie from the hot counter. He ate the pie and drank the coke. Then he stripped the cellophane wrapper from the packet of Winfields and took a cigarette and put it between his lips. Then he stopped. Kevin Chambers' leather wallet was sitting on the carpet beneath the glove box. He hadn't meant to take it but there it was. He picked it up. He lit his cigarette. It was too late to give the wallet back, even if he'd wanted to. He took out the driver's licence and studied the photograph. The resemblance was unmistakable. Was it possible he'd kept the wallet deliberately, knowing it would be useful to him? As a court reporter he'd heard cases defended on the grounds of unconscious rather than deliberate intention. Psychoanalysis recognised the possibility of unconscious intention even if the law didn't. Nick finished his cigarette, got out of the car and walked back to the shop. He thought of that morning in Hyde Park with Jess, when he'd pretended to be an expert on household cleaning products. The man with the questionnaire had bought every word of it. He was probably no more credulous than anyone else. People expected you to be who you said you were. It was one of the frailties of human nature. Or one of the virtues. The automatic door slid open. Somehow Nick knew that what happened in the next few minutes was going to change his life.

The bill for a box of black hair dye and a packet of disposable razors came to $22.74. Nick pushed Kevin Chambers' VISA card across the counter. He hadn't even had the chance to practise Chambers' signature, although a child could have copied the illegible scribble on the card. The acne-scarred shop assistant picked up the card. 'Cheque, savings or credit?'

'Credit,' said Nick.

The assistant hit a key on his touch-screen and swiped the card and slapped a cheap biro on the counter.

Nick picked up the pen. His heart raced as he dashed off the oversized 'C' followed by a horizontal slash that was supposed to represent the word 'Chambers'.

The assistant didn't even glance at the signature on the card, as Nick had somehow known he wouldn't.

Nick put the card back in the wallet and turned to leave.

'Don't you want this?' the boy asked.

Nick saw the hair dye and razors sitting on the counter.

The sly expression on the assistant's face made Nick think that he was going to ask for another look at the VISA card. Nick glanced at the fuzzy black-and-white image on the miniature closed circuit TV screen behind the counter – and for a moment had the unnerving feeling that the indistinct figure wasn't him at all, but Kevin Chambers.

As Nick drove south the weather became worse. The driver's door leaked. One of the windscreen wipers had lost its rubber. Twice he had to pull over until the rain eased.

He reached Ulladulla just after nine and decided to stop for the night. A few streets back from the harbour was a white-brick motel called The Willows. According to the flickering sign outside, the motel had rooms for fifty-five dollars. Two rows of units faced each other across a tarmac parking area bordered by straggly bottlebrush. There wasn't a willow in sight.

Nick parked the panel van and got out, leaving the dog frowning at him through the windscreen. There was some wasteland behind the motel. From the carpark it looked possible to drive straight across the wasteland onto a road that linked up with the highway. That was information worth knowing, if by any chance he had to leave in a hurry.

It took the proprietor a couple of minutes to respond to the bell. He was a man in his sixties, in green tracksuit pants and slippers and dressing gown. He emerged from his office yawning and rubbing his eyes. Frowning through a pair of half-moon spectacles, he looked Nick up and down. 'Where are you heading?'

'Sydney,' Nick answered.

'Yeah?' He squinted past Nick at the white panel van. 'Which one's yours then?'

'The panel van.'

'You'll be after a double then.'

'Sure. Why not?'

'Just the two of you is it?'

Nick didn't see that it was any of his business to correct the proprietor's mistake. On the contrary, he was happy to give the impression that he had company. If anyone was looking for Nick Carmody tonight they would expect him to be travelling alone.

'Just two, yes.'

The elderly proprietor stared at him, and Nick thought he was going to ask whether they were married, he and his mythical companion. Then he reached under the counter for the register. 'Double rooms are sixty-five. Breakfast extra.' He opened the register and turned it around for Nick to sign. 'Do you want breakfast?'

'No thanks. We'll be pushing off early.'

'Suit yourself.' He watched Nick write his details and then turned the register round. Even with his reading glasses on, he had to press his face almost against the page to read the words. 'Chambers,' he said, as if the name confirmed his worst suspicions.

'That's right.'

'Had a Chambers here some time back. Left a tap running. I had to have the carpet up.' The proprietor squinted over the top of his glasses. 'Wasn't you, was it?'

Nick held his gaze for a few seconds but the unfocused stare told Nick that the old man was almost blind. 'Not me,' he said. 'My first time down here.'

'Must have been someone else then.'

'Must have been.'

'Cost me nearly eight hundred dollars.'

'The carpet?'

'Smell wouldn't come out. Had to buy a new one.'

'That's too bad.'

'Chambers. I'm pretty sure that was his name. Polypropylene.'

Nick looked puzzled.

'The carpet. Polypropylene. Navy blue. You wouldn't want it in the house. No one cares, do they? What's on the floor. Could have sawdust and they wouldn't notice. Just come here to sleep. Someone walked off with a television set once.' He pointed across the forecourt. 'Number seventeen. Upstairs. Now they're all bolted to the wall.'

He waited for Nick to speak.

'It's a motel,' said Nick. 'I suppose—'

'Wife said I ought to have told the police. Malicious damage. Told her they wouldn't be interested. File a report and forget about it. Same with the television set. Asked me if it was insured. Next minute they're getting back in the car.' He paused, and started flicking through the register. 'I'm sure it was Chambers . . . Chalmers. Maybe that was it. Only eighteen months old.'

'The carpet?'

'We had them all done. Twenty-four units. Wife chose the colour.' He frowned and snatched a key from the board on the wall. 'Number seven,' he said. 'There's extra bedding in the cupboard if you want it.'

'Thank you.'

The old man handed him the key. 'There's no dogs, by the way.'

'Sorry?'

'Dogs.'

Leaning over the counter, the proprietor pointed to a small sign: NO DOGS, NO VISITORS, NO SMOKING.

'I can always smell a dog,' he said, tapping the side of his nose. 'The wife says it's a gift.'

'Don't worry,' said Nick. 'It sleeps in the car.'

The unit looked as if it hadn't been slept in for months. There were cobwebs in the corners. Four tea bags and a bowl of petrified white sugar sat on a plastic tray beside the kettle. Nick tried to open one of the windows but it was bolted shut and he couldn't find a key.

After locking the door he sat down to read the instructions on the box of hair dye. It all looked simple enough but the plastic gloves split and Nick was forced to improvise with a pair of supermarket bags. With the bags on his hands he couldn't avoid smudging dye on his temples. He studied the result in the bathroom mirror. He'd missed some of the roots but the overall effect was good enough. As he stood there he heard a knock on the door. He froze. Then he called out, as if to his nonexistent companion, 'I'll get it.'

Nick watched the doorknob turning silently in its socket. 'The TV in there is stuffed,' said a familiar voice. 'I could get another if you want.'

'Thanks for the offer,' said Nick. 'We don't watch much TV.'

'It wouldn't be any trouble. There's one in the office.'

'We'll be fine.'

'Fair enough. It's there if you want it.'

Nick slept with his clothes on, just in case. In case of what? Who exactly did he fear – the police? Michael Flynn? Or Kevin Chambers? Nick realised how much he didn't know about the man whose name he'd taken. Why had Chambers left his wallet and keys in an unlocked car next to a deserted beach? If the boxes of groceries were supplies for a journey, where was he going – and why? If he was going to report his car stolen, he would have done it by now. And if not, then what did he have to hide?

Nick began to regret having stopped for the night. Wouldn't it have been safer to have kept going? He could always have pulled over and slept in the car. Someone might have recognised the Valiant on its way through. If Kevin Chambers was a local, he would know who to ask. Nick was tempted to leave now, in the middle of the night, only he knew it would arouse suspicion – and he'd already given the motel proprietor ample reason to remember him. But Kevin Chambers wasn't local. According to his driver's licence Chambers lived in the western suburbs of Sydney. So what was he doing leaving his car unlocked in a deserted carpark at Seven Mile Beach?

Eventually he fell asleep – only to be woken by the sound of a car in the parking area, and by the slow arc of headlights, like the revolving beam of a lighthouse, shining through the windows. The car drove past, then came back. Nick looked at his watch. It was just after three in the morning. He rolled out of bed and pulled on his shoes and crawled to the window. The car was a white saloon – a Commodore, he thought. The last time he'd spoken to Danny Grogan was in a white Commodore.

The car stopped outside a block of units on the far side of the parking area but the engine was still running. Through a gap in the vertical blinds Nick thought he could see two people. He slipped the door latch. A figure – it looked like a woman but in the darkness Nick couldn't be sure – got out of the passenger seat and shut the door. Now he could see her high-heeled shoes. She walked around to the back of the car and took something from the boot, then opened the rear door on the driver's side and got in. Nick couldn't see the driver. The Commodore sat there with its engine running, not moving. Nick felt in his pocket for the keys to the panel van. Had the old man turned him in? He remembered the ruined carpet. Had Kevin Chambers really stayed here before?

Nick thought of Laura-May the skydiver from Sauk City, Wisconsin, who'd survived a fall of ten thousand feet without a parachute. The miraculously lucky happened every day. Why not the miraculously unlucky? He remembered the honey-mooning plane crash victims who'd been destined for the front page until they turned out not to exist. The splash that replaced them was about a Kempsey woman who'd run over a masked armed robber in the carpark of the local RSL, only to find that the robber was her own son.

As a junior reporter he'd suspected stories like that of being made up but they never were. Nick scoffed at the idea that age nurtured scepticism. Age nurtured belief, even in the unbelievable. Especially in the unbelievable. Who could have predicted a physical resemblance between Nick Carmody and Kevin Chambers – and yet the resemblance was a fact. Coincidence wasn't an unnatural contrivance but its opposite. It was what kept the world moving.

Finally the Commodore drove away, and Nick realised he'd been spooked by nothing more sinister than a furtive coupling in the back seat.

It was still dark when he crept out to the panel van with two supermarket bags full of dye-soaked newspaper. The dog stared at him wanly as he opened the car door: the sort of disappointed, reproachful morning-after look that reminded Nick of unhappy nights with Carolyn. He sat behind the steering wheel while the dog sloped off towards the waste ground, then clambered in beside him.

He'd told the old man he was on his way to Sydney, so he set off in that direction, then turned round and drove back, dipping his lights as he passed.

The sun was coming up. Before he came to Batemans Bay a road sign pointed to the Kings Highway. Beyond lay Braidwood; beyond that Queanbeyan and Canberra.

Nick pulled a copy of the *Daily Star* from a rack outside a service station. The splash said, OVERDOSE KILLS TYCOON'S SON. Beneath the headline was a picture of a body being removed from the back of an ambulance. Someone had tipped off the press: a switchboard operator, probably, or somebody at the hospital. An almost identical photograph was on the front page of the *Herald*. Nothing in the picture identified the corpse as that of Danny Grogan except, perhaps, the two bruised feet protruding from the blanket. Nick remembered the scene in the toilet cubicle at Central Court, which seemed now like a grim rehearsal for the final act of Danny's life.

The front-page story carried Michael Flynn's byline under a banner that said STAR EXCLUSIVE, although most of what he'd written had been taken from the files. The police, for once, were keeping their suspicions to themselves and for all Flynn's efforts his story added nothing to what had been on the radio a full twenty-four hours earlier: Danny had been discovered lying in the stairwell of a block of apartments in Bondi. The ambulance team had been unable to revive him. A used heroin syringe had been found with the body. Danny didn't appear to have been visiting anyone in the block and no witnesses had come forward to say who Danny might have been with on the night he died. Insofar as the evidence supported a theory, it was that Danny had simply walked in off the street and given himself a fatal shot of heroin.

Turning the page, Nick saw a photograph of himself under the headline: POLICE PROBE MISSING REPORTER LINK. It was the picture on Nick's staff ID card. Was that Perger's idea of a joke? If so, he'd done Nick a favour. The picture desk could have chosen from a selection of more or less flattering byline photographs, but Perger had picked a wild-eyed scowling mug shot that made

Nick look like a fugitive on a 'Wanted' poster. The chances of anyone – even Carolyn – recognising him from that photograph were slight. Strangely, there was no byline. It crossed Nick's mind that maybe Perger had bullied Sally into writing the story:

> *Daily Star* reporter Nick Carmody, who testified on Danny Grogan's behalf after Grogan's Audi TT coupe was caught speeding in Sydney's eastern suburbs, has gone missing.
>
> Carmody failed to show up for work yesterday and appears to have vanished from the house in Abercrombie Street, Chippendale where he has been living for the past few months.
>
> A friend of Grogan's from their school days at St Dominic's College, Carmody is known to have been in contact with the tycoon's son in the weeks before his fatal overdose.
>
> Colleagues at the *Star* are surprised at Carmody's disappearance. The police have been informed, but so far nothing has been found to connect Carmody with Grogan's death.
>
> Carmody is believed to be driving a red Toyota Camry, registration SVA 709. His dog is also missing.

There was, as Nick had anticipated, nothing in the story to justify the headline POLICE PROBE MISSING REPORTER LINK. If the nameless reporter was Sally then Flynn hadn't told her about the hit-and-run. Nevertheless, Nick was glad to have got rid of his car.

He skimmed the next few pages. Perger had gone overboard, as Nick knew he would, but most of the material was old hat – a tawdry retelling of Danny's life under the media spotlight. Had it been anyone but Danny, Nick would have been happy enough to play his part in the ritual cannibalising of a famous corpse, but now he was repelled. It was a pantomime of a human life and it made him cringe.

The *Herald* was more restrained in its coverage – the tabloids had always owned Danny Grogan – but restraint hadn't stopped the broadsheet from sending a photographer to snap his grieving mother in the hospital carpark.

Before driving off Nick looked at himself in the rear-view mirror. His face had subtly changed, although Nick had done nothing but dye his hair black. By altering a single feature he seemed to have initiated a deeper kind of metamorphosis – as if his face, the face of Nick Carmody, was adjusting to suit his new identity. Or was it something else: that Nick was looking at himself, for the first time, from the outside? He remembered the shock he had always felt when listening to himself on the radio. What he heard then was not his own voice but the strident, toneless voice of a stranger. In the mirror he saw, for a fraction of a second, a face he didn't recognise.

The flagpole of Parliament House loomed in the distance. Nick drove across the Commonwealth Avenue Bridge and parked the Valiant in a carpark near the National Convention Centre. He walked back towards the city centre. The black dye looked less convincing in daylight than it had under the dusty fluorescent light in the motel unit. He'd missed most of the roots and some of the ends. He needed a haircut.

The place he chose was a unisex hair salon sandwiched between a travel agent and a souvenir shop in the Jolimont Centre. Four of its five chairs were empty. A girl with black nails and black lipstick pinned an apron around his shoulders. 'My name's Jade,' she announced with a quizzical smile.

Nick asked for a number two cut. Jade opened a little zippered plastic bag with her name on it and picked out the necessary attachment, which she held up for his inspection – like a sommelier offering him wine to taste.

'So,' she said, lifting some strands of hair on her comb. 'Am I allowed to ask who was responsible for this – or is it a secret?'

'I was born with it,' said Nick.

'I mean the colour,' she said. 'Not the hair.'

'Oh,' he said. 'That was my girlfriend.'

'Really?' she answered, meeting his gaze in the mirror.

Nick began to regret not choosing Jade's taciturn colleague, who was snipping silently at a pensioner in a raincoat.

'All right,' he said. 'I did it. I thought I'd surprise her.'

'I bet you would have.'

'It was a spur of the moment thing. The instructions made it look easy.'

'The instructions always make it look easy.'

Nick watched her in the mirror. Jade didn't look like the sort of girl who spent her spare time reading the newspapers. She looked like the sort of girl who spent her spare time painting herself black.

'Why do you paint yourself black?' he asked.

'Don't you like it?' asked Jade. She held her fingernails out for him to admire. Nick admired them. His own fingernails were yellowish brown.

'You shouldn't smoke,' said Jade. 'It's not good for you.'

'I've quit,' he said. It was a short sentence but he never thought he'd hear it. Sometimes, admittedly, a person like him had uttered those words, but only in his dreams. Subconsciously, perhaps, Nick had longed to say them. But consciously, they were anathema – a betrayal of all the hours he'd spent (months in total – years, probably, by the time he retired) loitering on the pavement outside the *Daily Star*, struggling to keep a cigarette alight in the rain, or lurking like a burglar in the stairwell, keeping an ear out for the approach of the security man. Nick Carmody would never have given up smoking. Nick Carmody was going to die – prematurely, but with a perverse kind of satisfaction – with a cigarette between his fingers. But Kevin Chambers hadn't smoked a cigarette for nearly eighteen hours. Seventeen hours and forty-six minutes, to be exact.

'Excuse me for saying it,' said Jade, 'but you don't *smell* like someone who's quit smoking.'

'I quit last night,' he said. 'At ten past seven.'

Nick could tell that she didn't believe him; he only half-believed himself. She held up the mirror so he could see the back of his head. 'Short enough?'

'Fine,' he said. 'Just what I was after.'

'The colour still looks terrible,' she said. 'Are you sure you don't want me to fix it?'

'I can live with it. But thanks anyway.'

Jade took the nylon apron off his shoulders and shook the loose hair onto the floor. 'That's twenty dollars.'

It crossed his mind to give her fifty but a tip like that was the sort of gesture she wouldn't forget – and forgettability was a quality Kevin Chambers might need.

The dog was hungry. Nick found a supermarket and bought some tinned food and a plastic bowl. He sat and watched her eat. It was years since he'd spent more than three weeks away from his desk at the *Daily Star*. Somewhere in the personnel computer was a file showing his accumulated annual leave – nearly seven months, at the last count. Carolyn's idea of a holiday had been a fortnight in a luxury resort in Port Douglas or Fiji or Phuket. Nick thought of all the holidays he hadn't taken and all the trips he hadn't made and all the places he hadn't visited. He'd sacrificed them all to work and ambition. And for what? To find himself subbing stories about escaped alligators stalking the suburbs of Tupelo. He had five thousand dollars in his wallet. Five thousand dollars was a lot of petrol money.

He drove south to Cooma, north-west along the Snowy Mountains Highway, through Adaminaby and Kiandra all the way to the Murray River. It occurred to him that he didn't know where he was going – that if he made up his mind where he was going he would be able to choose the most direct route. But without a destination he could keep driving indefinitely. Maybe that was what he wanted.

Near the town of Boundary Bend (population 182) he swung off the Murray Valley Highway onto a dry-weather gravel road that took him to the junction with the Murrumbidgee.

He stood on the banks of the Murray, between the gnarled roots of a dead river gum, listening to the insect hum of irrigation pumps. On the far side of the river he could just make out the shape of a lone angler. The flow of the huge river seemed timeless, irreversible. He thought of the dead white explorers – Sturt, Mitchell, the canoeist Francis Cadell – encountering the river for the first time. He, too, was an explorer – an explorer of possibilities, of the possible lives and possible futures of Kevin Chambers.

As he returned to the panel van the raucous cry of a kookaburra burst from the branches above his head. The grey-hound sprinted ahead, as though reminded of its evenings on the track, then scampered back, as the sludge-green river lapped at its banks.

Bending down, Nick thumped his fist against the wing. A crescent-shaped shard of green glass was protruding from the offside front tyre. The broken remains of a bottle of Great Western champagne lay scattered on the gravel beneath the car.

Nick opened the tailgate. The spare was nearly bald but at least it had enough air in it to get him to a garage. He dragged it out and let it fall on the ground. The black plastic tool bag was lying in the well, tied with a length of striped nylon rope. There was another bag next to it – a dark-green household garbage bag sealed with silver gaffer tape. Nick untied the tool bag and took out the spanner and assembled the jack and dug away the loose gravel under the jacking point. The bolts were almost rusted on and it took him a long time to loosen them. Finally he got the wheel off and replaced it with the spare. He was about to throw the old wheel in the boot when he stopped. The dark green garbage bag was lying there and Nick was curious to know what was in it.

He picked it up. The bag was heavier than he was expecting. He carried it around to the front of the car and laid it on the bonnet. The contents shifted slightly as he tore off the silver tape. There were several items inside, wrapped in a strip of oiled cloth. Nick knew already what it was. The hairs on the back of his neck stood up as he gazed at the lovingly oiled pieces of a small-bore rifle. Next to it was a small box of .22 ammunition.

Nick didn't want to touch the gun. He re-wrapped the pieces and stuffed the bundle back where he'd found it and threw the old wheel on top and shut the tailgate. What did Kevin Chambers want with a gun?

He thought about the boxes of groceries. Then he searched under the front seats. He found a pair of binoculars in a case. They looked expensive. The leather handgrips were smooth and shiny from use. They smelt of sweat – and lubricating oil. Two brown elastic bands were stretched crosswise across the visor. Pulling it down, Nick found an Australian passport in the name Kevin Chambers.

He got out and examined the roof. The sun had broken down the enamel but just above the door he noticed scratches – the sort of scratches you'd get from hooking a searchlight to the edge of the roof. Nick got down on his hands and knees to look at the floor beneath the pedals. Red dirt was ground into the mat.

Chambers was a shooter. That explained the supplies. He drove into the bush to shoot kangaroos or wild pigs. Sometimes he shot at night and used a searchlight. It wasn't exactly a yuppie pursuit but out in Canley Vale pig-shooting wouldn't be an unusual hobby.

Hobby or not, Nick didn't want to keep the gun. For all he knew, it wasn't licensed. Even if it was licensed, he didn't like the idea of driving around in a stolen car equipped with a weapon and ammunition. He'd dispose of it – not here, where an angler might fish it up, but somewhere safe, where it wouldn't be found.

*   *   *

115

Nick had never heard of the *Sunraysia Daily* but there was his face the next morning – the wild-eyed mug shot from his staff ID card – scowling out from the top of page three. He was sitting in a gloomy corner of the public bar in the Grand Hotel in Mildura, nursing a bottle of Steinlager. The report consisted of six paragraphs in bold type under the headline FEARS HELD FOR MISSING REPORTER.

A car belonging to missing Sydney journalist Nick Carmody was found by police yesterday in a carpark at Seven Mile Beach, on the New South Wales south coast, close to Shoalhaven Heads.

The red Toyota Camry was located by an off-duty police officer from nearby Nowra. Despite a thorough search of the beach and dunes, no trace was found of Mr Carmody.

The ignition keys were found in the car, which was loaded with several boxes of groceries bought three days ago from the Grocery Drop in Nowra. The glove box contained two hundred dollars in cash. Recent tyre marks belonging to another vehicle suggest that Carmody might have met someone in the carpark. Broken glass near the scene indicates that the missing journalist could have been involved in a fight.

Friends and colleagues at the *Daily Star*, where until recently Carmody held the position of crime reporter, now hold grave fears for his safety.

'We're devastated,' said chief subeditor Jerry Whistler. 'Nicky's a top bloke and a great journo and we can't imagine what's become of him.'

According to the editor-in-chief of the *Daily Star*, Les Perger, Carmody was well-liked and had no enemies. 'No one I can think of,' said Perger, 'had any reason to do away with Nick Carmody.'

The picture looked, if anything, even worse than it had in the *Star* – a copy of a copy of a copy. It was like going backwards through some evolutionary chart: each successive image made Nick look coarser, more feral – and more guilty – than the one before.

The panel van was starting to fall apart. The exhaust fell off in a picnic area off the Sturt Highway. The gearbox felt ready to pack it in at any moment – sometimes, for no reason, it slipped into neutral and the engine revved madly for a few seconds before jerking back into gear.

Nick had driven for two days in the expectation that a destination would somehow emerge. Now it dawned on him that he was going to have to make a decision. Distance would protect him, but he knew he would feel safer in a crowd. He stopped thinking about heading west and started thinking about heading south: to Melbourne.

The gun was making him nervous. A few kilometres beyond Charlton, he stopped near a bridge and hurled it into the Avoca River. The bundle hit the water with a dull splash. Nick remembered a sultry summer morning in 1986, riding his bicycle in Centennial Park as police divers searched Busby's Pond after the murder of Sallie-Anne Huckstepp. If you dug deep enough, a park ranger had told him, you would find

the criminal history of Sydney entombed in the mud alongside the rusted bicycles and broken shopping trolleys.

Later, as dusk began to fall, Nick had the feeling that he was
being followed. He noticed a pale-coloured Ford station wagon
in his rear-view mirror. He was almost sure he'd seen the same
vehicle when he stopped for petrol in Wycheproof. It was a
common enough model but the colour – a sort of duck-egg
blue – stuck in his mind. He slowed down to let the other
driver pass but the station wagon seemed to slow down too.
When he speeded up, the station wagon appeared to do the
same. It might have been nothing. The distance between the
two vehicles slowly increased. It was almost dark when Nick
glanced in his mirror and realised that the station wagon wasn't
there anymore; it must have turned up one of the dirt tracks
he'd noticed earlier. A feeling of incredible relief swept over
him. His hands relaxed on the wheel. He drove for another
ten minutes before pulling over. He wound down the window
and breathed deeply. Was he going to break into a sweat every
time he saw another vehicle in his mirror? He picked up his
mobile phone. He had missed seventeen messages. A glance
would have told him who they were from but Nick didn't want
to know. Those messages were for Nick Carmody but he'd left
Carmody behind, in a carpark at Seven Mile Beach. He glanced
in the mirror. His dyed hair looked ridiculous. He wondered
how Kevin Chambers would look with his head shaved.

II

The impact sounded worse than it was – but it was bad enough. A busload of passengers with their faces pressed to the vandalised windows were staring at Nick as though he'd just come down in a shower of green sparks.

He was in a suburb called Box Hill, outside Our Lady of Sion College, and a bus had just run into the back of him. He didn't know how he happened to be in Box Hill and until a few seconds ago he'd never heard of Our Lady of Sion. He got out of the panel van and inspected the damage – which was less than he'd expected, although the tailgate had been pushed out of shape. The bus was unscathed except for a mildly deformed front bumper.

The bus driver looked younger than he did, and Nick felt guilty, as though the accident had been his fault, although the bus had run into him rather than the other way around. He resisted the impulse to apologise.

'Gee, mate, I'm sorry,' said the driver. 'Didn't you see me?'

Meaning what, Nick wondered – that it *was* his fault? He tried to force the tailgate back into place.

'You pulled out,' the driver explained.

'Did I?'

'Are you okay?'

'Sure.'

'Need me to call an ambulance?'

'I'm all right.'

'You look a bit shaken.'

'I'm fine. Let's just forget about it. I was going to get rid of the car anyway.'

The bus driver hesitated. He bent down to look at the deformed bumper. He ran his hand over the dent.

'I'd like to,' said the bus driver.

'Good—'

'Only the supervisor will want to see some paperwork.'

'Tell him I wouldn't stop. Tell him it was my fault.'

'It was your fault. You pulled out.'

'So you're in the clear.'

Nick was pushing down with all his weight on the damaged tailgate, which refused to shut.

The bus driver peered inside: 'How's the dog?'

'The dog's all right, thanks. We're both all right.'

'Greyhound, is it?'

Nick was beginning to realise why public transport always ran late. 'Yes. It's a greyhound.'

'Race, does he?'

'Used to. Not any more. She's retired.'

'She?' The bus driver walked around for a closer look. 'What's the name – if you don't mind my asking? I used to have a bit of a punt. Always liked a good bitch. You know what they say, don't you: it pays to follow a bitch in form.'

Nick gave up his attempts to close the tailgate. 'Listen, mate. I'd like to talk but I'm supposed to be somewhere. Is there any way we can fix this without bothering your supervisor?'

Two female passengers had left their seats and were walking towards them. The bus driver tried to wave them back. When they took no notice he physically herded them back up the steps. Nick seized his chance, jumping back in the car and pulling straight out into the traffic while the bus driver watched him with a look of disappointment bordering on betrayal.

'She's fucked. Pardon the Italian, but that tailgate is fucked.' The mechanic straightened himself up. He was about six and a half feet tall and hinged at several points. He put both hands in the small of his back and grimaced. 'I could try and hammer the fucker out but chances are it would still be fucked. You'd get water leaking in, rust, the works. Take my advice. It's not worth it.' He walked slowly around to the front. 'What's the engine like? Someone'll give you a few hundred for scrap if the engine's okay. If the engine's fucked you'll be lucky to get a hundred.' He hoisted the bonnet, held it up with one arm, glanced at the battery. 'New battery?'

'Newish,' said Nick.

'Give me a listen.'

Nick got in and started the engine.

'I've heard worse,' the mechanic said after listening for a few seconds. 'I don't mind giving you three hundred. Cash. Save you the trouble of taking it somewhere else.'

'What about five?'

The mechanic let the bonnet fall. 'What about four?'

Nick glanced over his shoulder at a motley assortment of used cars parked beside the workshop.

The mechanic wiped his hands on his overalls. 'Looking for something now, are you?'

'I could be.'

'What?'

Nick shrugged. 'What have you got?'

'Big? Small?'

'Small. Reliable. Not too expensive.'

The mechanic scratched his head, as if those specifications would be hard – even impossible – to meet. He put his hands on his hips. 'Reliable. Not too expensive.' He looked at the panel van. 'How much have you got to spend?'

Nick thought of the money in his pocket, the money Danny's father had given him. He couldn't afford to spend it all. Maybe he didn't need a car. But he'd had a car since he was seventeen. He'd be lost without a car. He noticed a scooter parked among the used cars beside the workshop.

'What about the scooter?'

'What about it?'

'Is it for sale?'

'It could be.' He looked Nick up and down. 'Ever ridden one before?'

'Not for a long time – why?'

'You don't seem like the kind of bloke who'd ride a scooter.'

'Really?' Nick was accustomed to defining himself – either on the telephone or by holding out a business card – and was curious to hear a stranger define him, even by what he was not. 'And what sort of bloke rides a scooter? In your opinion.'

'In my opinion?'

'Yes.'

The mechanic folded his arms. 'Students. Waiters.' He paused. 'Faggots.'

'How much?' asked Nick.

The mechanic unfolded his arms. 'How much did I say I'd give you for the Valiant?'

'Four hundred.'

'Call it a straight swap then. Yours for the scooter.'

At the last moment Nick hesitated. He didn't have the transfer papers. Maybe it would be safer just to drive the panel van into the bush and leave it.

The mechanic leaned back casually against the side of the car. 'I'm guessing,' he said, 'that you haven't brought the papers with you?'

'I forgot all about them,' said Nick.

There was a long pause. 'It's a bit of a risk buying a car without papers these days. I mean, you never know what the police might come nosing around. I don't suppose they'd be interested in a wreck like this but you can't be too careful.'

Nick knew all about risk, and how to compensate for it. 'Give me two hundred,' he said, 'and I'll forget about the scooter. I bet you could get two hundred just for the doors.'

The mechanic grinned. 'I knew you weren't a faggot.'

A bare scalp on a man under thirty-five both invited and rebuffed scrutiny. Was it an aggressive style statement, or hereditary and unavoidable – or was it the result of chemotherapy? Catching sight of himself in mirrors and shop windows, Nick had the feeling that baldness was going to suit Kevin Chambers. He noticed the looks he received from strangers as he walked around the city: wary, yes, but at the same time oddly impressed, even envious. Or was he just imagining it – projecting onto them the strange excitement he felt at slipping out of one life and into another? How many people, after all, got to do what he was doing? Millions dreamt of having a second chance, but how many had the nerve to go through with it – to simply disappear and start again?

And not a moment too soon. Michael Flynn had tracked down the female witness to the New Year's Eve hit-and-run. According to her, the driver of the Audi TT bore no resemblance to Danny Grogan. Nick swore out loud as he read the handful of paragraphs on page six of the *Daily Star*. It was as if he had written the story knowing that Nick would read it – as if Flynn was taunting him. Danny's father had got to the witness – or someone had – and made sure that the driver she remembered seeing looked nothing like Danny or his underage girlfriend. Nick wondered how much she'd been paid for her trouble. You could say one thing for Danny's father: he always paid. At the end of the story Flynn reminded the *Star*'s readers that his missing colleague, Nick Carmody, had admitted in court to driving Grogan's car on the night of the hit-and-run. Nick was no longer just a fugitive, but an outlaw.

He found himself rattling along Sydney Road in a number 19 tram, staring at the fabric shops bristling with bolts of pink and purple silk and the halal butchers with their awnings drawn against the sunlight. The dog was holed up in a motel room in West Maribyrnong, with a bag of Meaty-Bites and a bowl of water, behind a sign that said DO NOT DISTURB.

The tram halted outside an Afrocentric hair studio and Nick got off. He needed somewhere to live and this seemed like a good place to start looking. The pavements were busy but not crowded. Women carrying bags of shopping got on and off the tram without smiling. The street was lined with bargain shops and discount chemists and pawnbrokers. The population was largely immigrant and Nick got the feeling that people here minded their own business.

He crossed the road to a shop called Planet Real Estate. There were plenty of units for rent but Nick's eye was drawn to a picture of a weatherboard cottage whose front porch was being slowly strangled by a wisteria vine. The rent – $240 a week – was only a few dollars more than the agent was asking for a two-bedroom unit in a red-brick block of twelve.

Nick opened the door and walked inside. For all the ambition of its name, Planet Real Estate looked like a one-person operation. A man in his fifties in a corduroy coat was speaking on the telephone. Nick pointed to the window and asked whether the weatherboard cottage was still vacant.

Without removing the receiver from his ear the agent nodded and mouthed the word 'yes'. Nick asked for the address.

The agent put his hand over the mouthpiece. 'It's just around the corner. De Carle Street. Two minutes' walk.'

'Can I have a look?'

'Can you come back later?'

'I won't be here later.'

The agent pulled a face. Then he took his hand away from the mouthpiece. 'I've got to go,' he said. His voice sounded pained. Watching him, Nick guessed that the person on the other end of the line was his wife. 'I'll call you later,' the agent said, but seemed unwilling to end the call. (Was it his mistress, Nick wondered?) 'I'm not sure,' he said, looking now at Nick. 'Yes. I'll try.' Then he hung up.

'Sorry for interrupting,' Nick said.

Ignoring his apology, the agent rummaged in his desk drawer for the keys. Each set of keys had a cardboard tag and the agent had to read a dozen of them before he found the tag he was looking for. He followed Nick out of the office and turned the 'Open' sign to 'Closed' and locked the door behind them.

They stood side by side at the pedestrian crossing and waited for the walking man to turn green.

'Where are you from?' the agent asked.

Without thinking Nick answered, 'Sydney.'

The traffic stopped and they crossed the road.

'Sydney?'

'That's right.'

'Whereabouts in Sydney?'

'North.'

'You didn't like it?'

'It was okay. I felt like a change.'

The agent smiled, as if the thought of voluntary change amused him. They turned the corner into De Carle Street and walked in silence until Nick spotted the 'For Lease' sign across the street.

The weatherboard cottage looked as though it had been vacant for some time. The front garden was overgrown with weeds and there were rain-sodden brochures and snail-chewed envelopes all over the concrete path. The kitchen floor was covered with ancient green linoleum. A window pane on one side had been broken and there was a vague smell of wet carpet but there appeared to be nothing wrong with the house that a handyman couldn't fix.

'Why did the last tenant move out?' Nick asked.

The agent shrugged again. 'Why does any tenant move out?'

'Didn't they say?'

'Not to me,' said the agent, opening a cupboard and shutting it again. 'They left some things in the garage.'

'What sort of things?'

'Furniture. Nothing expensive. I think there's a small refrigerator in there.'

'Do you mind if I have a look?'

The agent unlocked the garage door. 'Go ahead.'

He was right. The abandoned furniture wasn't expensive but it was in pretty good condition and would enable Nick to move straight in. Apart from the refrigerator there was a formica kitchen table and two chairs, a 1950s veneer wardrobe, a small chest of drawers, and some cardboard boxes containing plates and cutlery.

The agent was waiting for him in the garden. 'So – do you think you might be interested?'

'I am interested,' said Nick.

'The rent is $240 a week.'

Nick didn't know if that was fair or not. It was the first place he'd looked at. He had three and a half thousand dollars left, and some cheques he didn't dare cash. He would have to start looking for a job.

'What about animals?' he asked.

'What about them?'

'I've got a dog.'

The agent shrugged.

'Make it $220 and I'll take it.'

The agent locked the house and they walked back to the office. As they waited at the pedestrian crossing he gave Nick his business card. His name was Terry Lawless and, like many real estate agents, he was a justice of the peace. Nick slipped the card into his wallet. A justice of the peace was exactly what Kevin Chambers was going to need.

That night Nick switched on the television in his room at the Sunset Lodge Motor Inn to see pictures of Harry Grogan and his ashen-faced wife, emerging from St John's Anglican Church in Darlinghurst after the funeral of their son.

The police had found nothing to indicate that Danny Grogan's overdose was anything other than accidental. Nick wondered how hard they had looked – how hard Harry Grogan had wanted them to look.

The *Age* was not the only newspaper to point out the 10 percent plunge in the share price of Grogan Constructions in the forty-eight hours that followed Danny's accident, and to calculate that – at least on paper – his son's heroin habit had cost Harry Grogan nearly one hundred million dollars.

Since Danny had never shown the slightest interest in running his father's company Nick found it hard to see why its shareholders were so shaken by his loss. Nevertheless Harry Grogan was forced to issue a statement coolly assuring them that the future of Grogan Constructions was 'unaffected' by his son's death. Was it true – or simply the sort of formulaic reassurance that timorous shareholders needed from time to time to steady their nerves?

The media seemed to have lost interest in the fate of Nick Carmody. At an internet cafe in the city, Nick found himself banished to the *Star*'s online archives. What could he expect? The life of a tabloid news story was about the same as the life of a carton of milk: at the *Star* news arrived with a use-by date. In the space of a week Nick Carmody had been transformed from news to its antithesis: old news.

*   *   *

If you believed the editorials in the *Daily Star* there were tens, even hundreds of thousands of people in Australia who never filed a tax return. In theory Nick knew it would be possible to survive like that for a while: as a non-person, an itinerant with no tax-file number, no driver's licence, no passport, no criminal record, no credit history. But sooner or later even a non-person would need to see a doctor and for that they would need a Medicare card – or a good reason for not having one. Once the non-person had found his or her way onto one database, they would be searched for on others. Some government computer in Penrith or Hobart or Bunbury would discover a driver's licence that had expired and never been renewed, a superannuation fund that hadn't been touched in years – and Nick Carmody would come magically back to life.

His years as a crime reporter had taught him that identity was a pyramid. At the apex of the pyramid was a passport or a driver's licence with a photograph; at the bottom were electricity bills and store cards. You could use document A to get document B, then use document B to get document C, until you had everything you needed to be a legitimate member of Australian society. He already had a passport in the name Kevin Chambers but the photograph was old and didn't look anything like Nick. He could report it stolen and attempt to get a replacement but it wouldn't be easy. Passport fraud was a hot issue these days and governments everywhere were cracking down. Besides, Nick had no use for a passport. He wasn't planning to travel anywhere. What he did need was a driver's licence with his own photograph, tangible proof of his new identity – a document he could trust implicitly, and which he could use to obtain other documents.

Nick wasn't sure how much longer he could go on using Chambers' credit card. He'd assumed that Chambers would cancel the card as soon as he discovered it was missing. He'd even rung the stolen cards hotline, pretending to have found it, only to discover that Kevin Chambers' card had never been reported lost. Since then Nick had used the credit card only once, at a supermarket in the city, where there was no risk of being remembered.

It worried him that Chambers hadn't cancelled the card. If his plan was to come after Nick then the credit card would tell him where to start looking. The sooner Nick stopped using it, the better. Was Kevin Chambers the kind of man who took the law into his own hands? Nick hadn't forgotten the gun, and he guessed that Chambers wouldn't have forgotten it either.

On Friday afternoon Nick was to hand over his bond money and the balance of the first month's rent in advance, and in return receive the keys to number 75 De Carle Street. On Thursday morning he used Kevin Chambers' driver's licence to hire a car from Avis in Elizabeth Street. The man behind the counter was only interested in his credit card and didn't even look at the photo on the licence. Nick would return the car undamaged and with a full tank of petrol, then the credit card imprint would be destroyed. He would settle the bill with cash and no one would be any the wiser. After hiring the car Nick drove to a chemist's in St Kilda and had some passport photographs taken. In the afternoon he drove out to Coburg.

Terry Lawless had his back to the door. He was transferring files from one grey metal cabinet to another. At the sound of the bell he turned round. He looked surprised to see Nick.

He stopped what he was doing and walked to his desk and glanced sheepishly at the calendar.

'Didn't we say Friday?'

'We did say Friday.'

'Is there a problem?'

'Maybe, Terry. I hope not. You see . . . I've just lost my wallet.'

Lawless sat down. 'Lost?'

'I was robbed. This morning. Someone picked my pocket.'

'That's terrible. You've reported it to the police?'

'Of course. But what are the police going to do?'

Nick could see Lawless working through the implications in his head, trying to discern whether this was just an inconvenience or something more serious.

'What was in the wallet?'

'Some cash. All my cards. My driver's licence. Everything.'

'You must cancel the cards.'

'It was the first thing I did.'

Lawless breathed a sigh of relief. 'How much money was in the wallet?'

'It's not the money I'm worried about. It's my driver's licence. I can't work without it.'

'You must apply for a new one. They will understand. People lose wallets all the time.'

'They'll want some ID,' said Nick. 'The trouble is, all my stuff's in Sydney. If I can't arrange things from here I'll have to go back for it. I won't be able to take the house.' He sat down. 'Unless you can help me, Terry.'

Lawless didn't say anything but Nick could guess what he was thinking. He'd already let slip that the cottage in De Carle Street had been in his window for nearly six months. Now that he'd spent money on having the carpets cleaned and replacing the broken window, he couldn't afford to lose the lease.

The agent shifted awkwardly in his seat. 'How?'

'You're a JP. You can speed things up for me.'

Lawless smiled modestly. 'I don't think so, Mr Chambers.'

Nick unzipped his rucksack and took out a form he'd downloaded from an internet cafe near the university. 'This is an application for a replacement licence.'

'Yes,' said Lawless, glancing at the form. 'I've seen this form.'

'All you need to do is sign the documents and say you've seen them.'

'They must be original documents.'

'That's the problem, Terry. I need a new driver's licence. The old one was stolen. If I can prove to you that I had the licence, will that be good enough for you?'

Lawless looked agitated. 'I don't know, Mr Chambers. I am a justice of the peace.'

'That's why I came to you, Terry. Because you're a justice of the peace. And you know me. And after all the trouble you've gone to I'd hate not to be able to take the house.'

Nick unfolded the yellow duplicate copy of the Avis car rental agreement and laid it on the desk. 'Here's my licence number. Address. Date of birth. Obviously I had the licence with me when I rented the car this morning. All you have to do is pretend you've seen it. I'll say the old one was damaged. Nobody is going to bother checking.' He took out the envelope containing his new passport photograph. 'Of course,' he added casually, 'you'll need to certify that it's me in the picture.'

After reading the form, Lawless said, 'I'm supposed to see the licence.'

'But the licence was stolen. That's why I'm here.'

Lawless attempted to push the form back across the desk. 'I think maybe you should ask someone else to do this.'

'Who else can I ask? I've come to you because I trust you. I can hardly expect a total stranger to vouch for me. It's not as if I'm trying to deceive anyone. If someone hadn't stolen my wallet I wouldn't be wasting my time filling in forms.'

'You are certain the licence was stolen?'

'Yes.'

Lawless picked up the passport photograph and stared at it. 'It certainly looks like you.'

'Of course it's me. I only had it taken an hour ago.'

Lawless put the photograph down and picked up the form and read it again.

Sensing that he was going to get what he wanted, Nick felt guilty for his crude emotional blackmail. Terry Lawless seemed like a nice man: decent, old-fashioned, pedantic, and anxious to be liked. On the desk was a framed picture of a younger Terry and a pretty woman in a summer dress and sun hat. Nick remembered the phone call he'd witnessed the last time he was in the office. He picked up the photograph and heard himself ask, 'Is this your wife?'

A rueful look came over the agent's face. 'Yes,' he murmured. 'Myself and my wife.'

Nick put the photograph back on the desk and for a few moments they both stared at it.

'Yes,' the agent said at last. 'I think perhaps I can do as you ask. It is only a small request and the alternative is . . . ' His voice petered out as if he wasn't exactly sure what the altern-ative was.

'Thank you,' said Nick. 'You've saved me a lot of trouble.'

Lawless smiled weakly as he reached for his pen. 'It is not your fault, after all, that your wallet was stolen.'

Nick watched in silence as Lawless copied the number of Kevin Chambers' driver's licence from the duplicate rental agreement and signed the form and passed the pen to Nick so that he could witness his signature at the bottom. Then he certified the photograph and handed everything back across the desk.

'Until tomorrow then,' said Nick, standing up.

'Yes,' Lawless agreed. 'Until tomorrow.'

A fortnight later Kevin Chambers' replacement driver's licence was delivered to his door. The next day a letter arrived from Telstra confirming the details of his twenty-four month phone plan. Nick wrote immediately to the New South Wales Registry of Births, Deaths and Marriages, quoting Kevin Chambers' date of birth and requesting a copy of the birth certificate he claimed to have lost while moving house. As proof of his identity he sent certified photocopies of Chambers' new driver's licence and the letter from Telstra. On the day Chambers' birth certificate arrived by registered post from Sydney Nick used it to open a savings account at the Coburg branch of the Commonwealth Bank.

Already the name Nick Carmody seemed to belong to someone else – a colleague or an acquaintance he'd become used to not seeing. It joined the thousands of names that belonged to a past that was no longer his.

He remembered the first time he'd read his own byline in the *Star* – and his horror when he realised the story

(EXTINCT TIGER BLAMED FOR MAULED SHEEP) was by a different Nick Carmody, an elderly stringer who filed occasional stories for the paper from Tasmania. Seeing his name over some-body else's work had made his head spin. It seemed incred-ible that Nick Carmody could be a nineteen-year-old cadet journalist living with his parents in Maroubra as well as a seventy-two-year-old retired Tasmanian university lecturer. Nick felt that day as if something had been stolen from him – not just his name but his future. In a moment of reckless pretension he adopted the name of his then-favourite writer, the Polish émigré author of *Under Western Eyes* and *The Secret Agent*. For a few months he laboured under the byline 'By Nick Conrad Carmody' until the retired lecturer died suddenly in his bed and Nick was free to become himself again.

You expected rain in Melbourne. But the place was dying of thirst. It was a city of parched lawns and dying trees and houses cracking from lack of moisture.

During his walks around Coburg Nick often passed a two-storey, honey-brick, colonnaded mansion in Wattle Grove, on the other side of Sydney Road. The house nestled behind a wrought-iron gate and a row of miniature fir trees that drew attention to its extravagance rather than concealing it. Sometimes Nick saw a taxi parked outside and now and then a heavily built, dark-haired, middle-aged man getting out of the taxi or preparing to drive it. Clearly the owner was rich enough to drive the taxi only when he felt like it.

Driving a taxi, it seemed to Nick, was the sort of practical, anonymous job that might suit Kevin Chambers for a while. He still had enough cash, he discovered, to sign up for an eight-day course with the CABS4U Driver Academy in Port Melbourne.

On the day he finished the course, Nick pressed the aluminium security buzzer beside the wrought-iron front gate of the mansion in Wattle Grove. The taxi was parked outside. A grey-haired man on a stepladder was shaping the miniature fir trees with electric shears.

The voice that answered the buzzer sounded foreign – Russian or East European, Nick thought.

'Homolka,' he said, as if answering a telephone.

'My name is Kevin Chambers,' said Nick.

'What can I do for you, Mr Chambers?'

Homolka listened courteously before inviting Nick to come in.

Homolka was a Pole who'd taught economics at the University of Warsaw before escaping the Iron Curtain in the boot of a Trabant. Capitalism had been good to him. In twenty years he had made himself a rich man. As well as owning a taxi, he'd bought several run-down properties in suburbs of Melbourne that would soon become desirable.

House by house Homolka recounted the purchase price and current market value of his investment properties as he and Nick sat on the front porch, watching the old man on the stepladder. It seemed important to Homolka for Nick to know exactly how much he was worth.

'You're a lucky man,' said Nick.

'All mortgage, of course,' replied Homolka. 'Otherwise no need for taxi.'

He smiled and Nick smiled back.

'Good money for old communist, yes?'

'I thought it was only old communists who made money in your country.'

Homolka laughed, then frowned, then laughed again. 'You – what – thirty years old?'

'Close enough.'

'How long you drive taxi?'

'I won't lie to you, Mr Homolka. I've just finished the course.'

'What course?'

'CABS4U Driver Academy.'

'I never heard of this place.'

'It's in Port Melbourne.'

'These people teach you drive taxi?'

'More or less.'

'Promise job afterwards?'

'Yes.'

Homolka said something to the old man on the stepladder, and Nick realised that the gardener, too, was Polish. They exchanged some heated opinions before the old man switched off his electric shears and descended the stepladder and resumed the job with a pair of hand clippers. Then Homolka looked sideways. 'Homolka teach you,' he said. 'Five hundred dollars.'

'Thanks,' said Nick. 'But I'm qualified now.'

'Four hundred fifty,' said Homolka. 'Cash.'

Nick didn't reply. He wasn't sure whether the Pole was pulling his leg or whether Homolka was serious about charging him to learn what he already knew. After an awkward silence Homolka took a packet of cigarettes out of his pocket and asked, 'What is father?'

Nick had been waiting for this question. He'd been waiting

for it from the moment he drove away from the service station in Nowra. If he was to create a future for himself as Kevin Chambers he would also need to create a past. Not just a date of birth but a family, a history of friends and lovers he could memorise and recite at will. He would have to immerse himself in the intimate details of an imaginary life. It was like an actor's exercise, only Nick couldn't afford to make a mistake.

'My father drove a bus.'

Homolka shrugged and offered Nick a cigarette, which he declined. 'Dead now?'

'Yes.'

'And mother?'

'She lives in Scotland. A village called Crail. They divorced.'

'Brothers and sisters?'

'None.'

'Wife?'

'I'm not married.'

'Live alone then,' said Homolka, looking sympathetic but at the same time pleased. 'Night shift no problem.'

'I've got a dog,' said Nick.

'Dog okay,' said Homolka. 'Dog stay at home. Bark at burglars. You come home. Nothing stolen.'

'I hadn't thought of it like that.'

'Not much traffic at night,' said Homolka. 'Roads empty. Work hard make good money. Save up buy taxi plates make more money. Buy house get family watch children grow up.' He held out his fleshy hands as if these instructions had merely to be followed, like the steps in a cooking recipe, for the result to be achieved. And for a moment Nick wondered whether life really was – or could be – that simple. He thought of his own life and of the things he'd wanted that had been snatched away, or had turned out not be the things he wanted after all. Homolka patted him on the thigh. 'Simple, yes?'

The Pole walked across the lawn and issued some instructions to the old man. Then he returned and tossed Nick the keys to the taxi. 'Come, Kevin Chambers,' he said. 'I give you test.'

Later, having successfully delivered Homolka to the domestic terminal at Tullamarine Airport, and then to a hotel in Dandenong, and finally to a small house Homolka owned in Berembong Drive, Keilor East, Nick pulled up outside the honey-brick mansion in Wattle Grove. He switched off the engine and took out the keys and handed them to Homolka.

'You drive too slow,' said the Pole, opening his door. 'But I give you job.'

You read about transplant patients wanting to know whose organs they carry inside them: or wishing they didn't know (the born-again Christian whose donor was an atheist; the Boer farmer whose new heart is black). You read about them in waiting rooms, in showrooms – and wonder what it must be like, to feel the beat of another person's heart, to look through someone else's eyes. Does the transplanted organ surrender its identity to the new owner, or does the previous owner live on inside the host?

Nick found himself wondering more than ever what had become of Kevin Chambers. In return for taking his panel van Nick had left Chambers a couple of hundred dollars and the keys to a ten-year-old Toyota Camry, but Chambers had neglected to take either. Nor, apparently, had he reported the theft of his own vehicle. Perhaps he'd wanted the panel van to be stolen. A vehicle like that would have little resale value but it might still be insured for several thousand dollars. But that didn't explain the boxes of groceries. Nowra was a long way from Canley Vale. It seemed obvious to Nick that Kevin Chambers had been preparing to go on a trip. Was he, too, running away from something?

He began to feel a strange empathy for this man he'd never met, whose name and car and wallet he'd stolen. He'd thought of Kevin Chambers as an abstraction: a name and a date of birth, sixteen embossed digits on a credit card and some property left in the back of a panel van. But Chambers wasn't an abstraction. Nor was he flesh and blood. He was something in between – a vague presence that sometimes felt so real that Nick could almost hear the sound of his breathing. There were nights when he imagined Chambers sitting in the back seat of the taxi as he drove home at 3 a.m. from Frankston or Craigieburn with the radio blaring and the heater turned up. Or traipsing behind as he walked the dog around Mayer Park. But when he looked around, there was nobody there.

Now and then he detected a more palpable shadow: a dark-haired man in a fawn jacket who may or may not have been following him. But he never saw more than a fleeting glimpse – like a glimpse of Hitchcock in a Hitchcock movie: a bald fat man getting off a tram or buying a newspaper or earnestly studying an object in a shop window. In a city of four million strangers, Nick told himself, there must be dozens of dark-haired men with fawn jackets.

*   *   *

142

On Friday afternoons at half past three Nick collected a pensioner named Goldsworthy (he'd never confided his first name and Nick had stopped asking) from a block of red-brick flats in Glen Huntly Road, Elwood and drove him to the Cricketers Bar at the Windsor Hotel, where Goldsworthy sat over a pot of Melbourne Bitter and watched the television and occasionally found someone to talk to until, sometime after nine o'clock, Nick came to fetch him. Goldsworthy was old and truculent: most weeks he didn't say a word in either direction but sat with his gnarled and liver-spotted hands folded in his lap, frowning at the meter.

Today being Friday, at 3.22 p.m. Nick was speeding along St Kilda Road en route to Glen Huntly Road. Although the late shift started at two o'clock, Nick usually took it easy for the first hour, knowing he'd be driving flat out for most of the night. He took his regular route along Barkly Street and turned left into Mitford Street at the intersection with Blessington.

He had just accelerated from a roundabout when a pink bubble car pulled out ahead of him. Nick had time to brake but not to avoid the collision. The impact was slight enough for him to think no serious damage had been done, but when he got out of the taxi he found the road strewn with shards of broken plastic and fragments of rubber hose.

The pink bubble car's vented boot lay on the road, exposing the coiled entrails of its tiny rear-mounted engine. Nick watched in a kind of trance as a short, dark-haired woman in a peasant dress got out of the car, which had slewed diagonally across the road and was now pointing towards the driveway from which it had emerged moments earlier. At least, that was where it seemed to emerge from. In fact, though Nick could see what had happened, he wasn't sure how it had happened. Had he collided with her – or had she collided with him?

The woman was shaking her head. 'What were you playing at?'

Homolka had lectured him numerous times on the importance of never admitting fault for an accident.

'I'm sorry,' said Nick. 'It was my fault.' He felt her gaze on his skull. He was accustomed to it by now – a shaved head turned every stranger he met into a phrenologist. 'Are you all right?' he asked

'Pardon?'

'Are you hurt?'

'I learnt to drive in this car.'

Nick stared at the roof. The painting had been done by hand: he could see the clumsy brushstrokes. There was a shawl over the back seat. For a second or two he thought he recognised the woman but she showed no sign of recognising him.

'I didn't see you pull out,' he said.

'It's a fifty zone. You were going too fast.'

Nick knew he hadn't been driving at more than forty kilometres per hour when the accident happened, but what was the point of arguing? He shrugged and held up his hands. He'd already accepted guilt – what more could he say?

It was less than two minutes since the accident and already a tow truck was on the scene: a low-slung, chrome-fronted predator drawn by the smell of engine oil. Nick could feel the gurgle of its V8 as it pulled up behind him. The tow-truck driver, a bear of a man in green overalls and Blundstones, took one look at the bubble car and said, 'That's a write-off, sweetheart.'

'I'm not your sweetheart,' said the woman.

The tow-truck driver shrugged. 'Which of youse is paying for the tow?'

'He is,' she said.

The driver returned to his truck and got a clipboard and came back and handed it to Nick. 'Name. Address. Insurance company.' He looked sideways. 'What about you, love?'

'What about me?'

'Am I taking you too?'

'No.'

The tow-truck driver lit a cigarette without offering them around. 'If there's anything you want,' he said, 'you'd better take it now.'

She opened the door and snatched the shawl off the back seat.

The tow-truck driver secured the mangled car with chains and pulled up his ramps and climbed into his cab. 'So what's it to be?' he called out. 'Is the lady coming with me?'

'No,' she answered. 'She's not.'

They listened to the V8 clear its throat and instinctively stepped back as the tow truck roared away down Mitford Street.

'I suppose we should be exchanging details,' said Nick.

'That's what normally happens.' She searched her handbag for a pen and paper. The accident, Nick couldn't help feeling, had been as much her fault as his, but he felt the urge to reassure her that it was just a car and no one was hurt and everything was going to be all right.

'I've got a pen in the taxi,' he said.

She followed him to the car and stood there while he telephoned Goldsworthy to say he'd be late.

'My name is Alison Lake,' she said. 'I live at 99 Drummond Street, Carlton.'

'Kevin,' said Nick. 'Kevin Chambers, 75 De Carle Street, Coburg.'

They exchanged phone numbers and insurance details.

'I'm supposed to be somewhere,' she said. 'Are you for hire?'

'If you don't mind sharing.'

He told her about the old man in Glen Huntly Road – and had the odd feeling that she wasn't listening, that she was nodding politely while thinking about something else. He used to do it himself with passengers who wouldn't stop talking. Once you'd mastered the art of not listening you could tell when to nod simply by the tone of voice.

'Where can I take you?'

'Drop me at the Windsor. I can walk the rest of the way.'

'Once I've dropped the old boy I can take you wherever you want to go. It'll stop me feeling guilty about the accident.'

'What makes you think I want you to stop feeling guilty about the accident?'

Nick shrugged. 'What if I promise to keep feeling guilty?'

'Just drop me at the Windsor.'

They drove for a while in silence. Nick could feel her watching him, though she looked away whenever he glanced in the mirror.

'How long have you been driving a taxi?'

'Not long.'

'Is mine the first car you've written off?'

There was a half-smile on her face – enough to make Nick think they might be getting on quite well, all things considered.

'I guess it would be,' he said.

'I hope it's not going to cost you a lot of money.'

'So do I.'

'What did you do before you drove a taxi?'

'Oh,' Nick began slowly, 'this and that.'

'Isn't that what people say when they've just got out of prison?'

'I thought they said, "I got these tattoos in Thailand."'

'Very funny.'

Of course Nick had answered the same question dozens of times before, but never to anyone who mattered. He'd become adept at improvising colourful histories for the entertainment of Saturday night drunks and jetlagged passengers driving home from the airport. It was a challenge: to make the story interesting but plausible, to keep the details consistent and avoid contradicting himself. Not that most of them would have noticed if he had contradicted himself. They didn't care – he was just a bald-headed man driving a taxi – and he didn't care either. It wasn't as though anyone was going to make an official complaint because they didn't believe the cabbie's life story. But something in the way she looked at him made him think that Alison Lake just might matter, that the story he told her was one he ought to remember, because she would remember it too.

'I've been working in the west,' he said. 'Driving trucks mostly. I lived in Karratha for a while.'

'And?'

'I kicked around up north.'

'Doing what?'

'Prawns.'

'Eating them? Cooking them?'

'Trawling for them. In the gulf.'

'Perhaps I've eaten a prawn you trawled.'

'I'm sure you'd remember. I always signed them. Just below the ear.'

'I didn't know prawns had ears.'

Nick turned the corner into Glen Huntly Road. Goldsworthy was waiting, as usual, on the pavement. He registered Alison's presence in the taxi but didn't comment.

Nick dropped the old man outside the Windsor Hotel and waited for Alison to get out. It surprised him how anxious he was to see her again. He sensed that she felt the same but wasn't going to say it. One of them had to say something. He took a business card from the clip on the dashboard and passed it back between the seats. 'If you ever need a taxi,' he said, 'Night work a speciality . . . unusual jobs welcome.'

She stared at the card for a few moments before tucking it inside her bag. 'I'll call you,' she said, 'if there's any problem with the insurance.'

It was a couple of weeks before the phone rang. Nick was in the shower. He got out and tied a towel around his waist and stood dripping in the hallway. 'Hello?'

'It's Alison,' she said.

When he didn't answer immediately, she said, 'You ran into my car.'

'Alison. Yes. Of course.'

'I hope I'm not interrupting anything.'

'No. Of course not.'

'I'd like to ask you a favour.'

'What sort of favour?'

'I need a new car. The insurance company has given me some money. I thought you might want to help since it was your doing.'

He forgave her ironic tone. 'Help how, exactly?'

'By giving me your advice. About what to buy.' She paused. 'You must know something about buying cars?'

It sounded suspiciously like a wind-up – a practical joke of the sort that Jerry Whistler liked to organise for the *Star*'s annual Christmas party. 'A bit,' he said, warily. 'I wouldn't call myself an expert.'

'As long as you know more about cars than you know about prawns I'm sure we'll get by. Prawns don't have ears. They receive sensory information via nerves coming from muscles and the body wall that sense vibrations and small water movements. Prawns don't have a nose either, but they have olfactory receptors that can detect chemicals in the water.' She paused. 'Is there anything else you want to know – or can it wait until we meet?'

'I'm pretty sure it can wait. When do you want to look for the car?'

'What about tomorrow morning?'

Tomorrow was Saturday. Nick would be driving the taxi until 2 a.m. On Saturdays he rarely dragged himself out of bed before midday. 'Tomorrow morning's fine,' he said.

'I'd offer to pick you up, only . . . '

'Your car was involved in an accident. I remember.'

'There's a car yard just down the road, near the markets. I saw a nice red car through the fence. We could see if it's still there.'

'Red?'

'Dark red. Chianti red.'

'Oh, that sort of red. What time?'

'We could have brunch first.'

'We could.'

'Let's meet outside Jimmy Watson's.'

'Lygon Street?'

'So they do teach you your way around?'

'Sort of.'

'Is half past ten too early?'

'I'll be there.'

Nick put the phone down and walked into his bedroom and stared at the IKEA clothes hanger. There was nothing on it that he really wanted Alison to see him wearing. An iron would have widened his options, but not significantly. Driving a taxi was a stressful occupation, but it didn't offer much in the way of exercise. Since giving up smoking he'd put on three or four kilos. He thought of the Italian linen jacket and three crumpled suits he'd left hanging in a wardrobe in Abercrombie Street. None of them would fit him now. It seemed appropriate that Nick Carmody's old clothes shouldn't fit Kevin Chambers.

He caught the number 19 tram into the city and walked around the mall until he saw a plain white cotton T-shirt on a rack outside a shop. He looked at the price tag. Nick Carmody would never have spent so much money on a T-shirt – but Nick Carmody wasn't buying it.

According to his watch he was seven minutes early. It was 10.23 a.m. and Alison was already walking towards him, speaking to someone on her mobile phone. She was wearing a black top and leggings, with a cream cardigan tied around her shoulders. Her hair was pulled up in a French knot that was already coming undone. She looked surprised to see Nick waiting for her.

'Very smart,' she said, admiring the new T-shirt. 'White suits you.'

'Thanks.'

She fingered the material. 'Nice cotton. You'll have to hand-wash it, of course. If you chuck it in the machine it'll be ruined.'

'I haven't got a machine.'

'That's all right then.' She paused. 'What do you feel like?'

'It's your invitation,' said Nick. 'You choose.'

They walked up the street until Alison found a place she liked.

'You've done something to your hair,' said Nick.

'I've washed it.'

'No, I mean—'

'You mean I've tied it up in this sort of corkscrew thing that looks quite nice in theory except that it's already falling apart because it hasn't got enough clips to hold it together.'

'That's exactly what I meant.'

She glanced at his naked scalp. 'There's a lot to be said for the low-maintenance option.'

There was one table left outside. They took it.

'You know what I do,' Nick said, 'but I don't know what you do.'

'I'm with Qantas.'

'Go on.'

'I fly to exotic places, sleep in ordinary hotels, then fly home.'

'Where do you fly?'

'Wherever I'm told to fly. Mostly Asia at the moment. Sometimes Los Angeles. London when I get the chance.'

'It sounds glamorous.'

'You're right. It does sound glamorous.'

'But it isn't?'

Alison shrugged. 'One foreign city is much like another if you spend all day sleeping.'

'And do you?'

'Sometimes. It depends.'

'On what?'

'The city. The hotel. The state of my feet. I'm thinking of the smoked salmon omelette. What about you?'

'Scrambled eggs.' Nick folded his menu and put it down on the plate. 'So where was your last trip?'

'Los Angeles.'

'Did you enjoy it?'

'I stayed two nights and never left the hotel.'

'Because of the state of your feet?'

She caught the waiter's eye and beckoned him over. 'Because I was scared of getting shot.'

'Now that's what I call an occupational hazard.'

'You can laugh. Gangland starts right outside the hotel lobby. You think St Kilda on a Saturday night is dangerous. I take my life in my hands to go and buy a bagel for breakfast.'

'Sorry.'

'It's not all smiling and passing out immigration cards.' She lifted her bag onto her lap. 'I brought some bits of the paper. Is there anything you want to read?'

Reading the paper was the last thing Nick felt like doing but for Alison it seemed to be part of the ritual.

'Here,' she said, not waiting for him to make his decision. 'You have the news.' It sounded curiously like a challenge before she added, 'I want the magazine.'

They read for a couple of minutes in silence. Once again, Nick caught the odd glance that suggested she was more interested in watching him than she was in reading the magazine. After a while she turned to the astrology column at the back. 'I don't believe it,' she said. 'But I like to read it anyway. What sign are you?'

Nick froze. He'd forgotten Kevin Chambers' birthday. He'd written down his date of birth numerous times – but now that he needed it, it wasn't there. He couldn't even remember the month. If Alison had been a stranger in his taxi he could have told her anything he wanted. But she wasn't a stranger, and he didn't want her to be.

'Come on,' she said. 'I'm waiting.' Her finger was poised over the page. 'Just tell me the date.'

Nick tried in vain to drag the date from his memory. 'Shouldn't I know what I'm revealing first?' He struggled to conceal the note of panic in his voice. Out of the corner of his eye he spotted the pot-bellied waiter coming towards them with a big white plate in each hand. 'That was quick,' he said, sweeping his part of the newspaper off the table.

A look of mild annoyance flashed across her face. Then she smiled, as if it had all been a game.

'Signorina,' murmured the waiter as he delivered her smoked salmon omelette into the space vacated by the magazine. He presented Nick's scrambled eggs with a barely audible, 'Signor'.

'Thirty-three,' she said, 'and still a signorina.'

Nick had imagined she was younger. After Carolyn's self-consciousness Alison's lack of inhibition felt exhilarating – and dangerous.

'You're shocked,' she said.

'No – of course I'm not.'

'You thought: twenty-five at the most.'

'Twenty-one,' said Nick. 'If you really want to know.'

She smiled. 'It's spending half your life at ten thousand metres. It retards the ageing process.'

'Is that true? I always thought it was the other way around.'

'You see – it's a myth that taxi drivers know everything.'

A visit to the bathroom as they waited for more coffee gave Nick the chance to check his driver's licence. His birthday was 7 April. When he returned Alison was immersed in a profile of the leader of the opposition's ex-wife. She looked up as Nick sat down. 'I always knew he was a bastard.'

Nick glanced at the photograph. 'She's not telling that story again of how he promised to stay at home and look after the kids in return for her letting him do his doctorate.'

'She says this is the first time she has ever told anyone.'

'She's lying. She tells the same story to everyone who interviews her.'

Alison studied him across the table.

'And how would you know that?'

Nick blushed. In his eagerness to show off he'd almost given himself away as a journalist. 'I must have read it half a dozen times.'

She frowned and turned the page. 'Ex-wives always get a raw deal from journalists – especially female ones.'

Nick picked up the news section. Another gangster had

been shot dead – executed in a crowded tapas bar by a man in a balaclava helmet – and the *Age* had given nearly half its front page to the story. The chief crime reporter had written a long comment piece and the graphics department had supplied a helpful timeline of previous executions. Nick turned the page to read the spill. Before he could find it, his eye fell on another story. He stopped with the cup of coffee halfway to his mouth. The headline said, LIGHTNING KILLS MAN. It was an agency piece, a handful of paragraphs pulled off the wire to fill an awkward space.

A man named Kevin Michael Chambers, thirty-four, had been found incinerated in his car – a white Holden utility – on a semi-rural property near Camden, south-west of Sydney. Camden wasn't far from Canley Vale – about thirty minutes by car. The incident sounded like a freak of nature: a lightning strike had ignited the petrol tank. The vehicle was old and both door locks were broken. Chambers had burnt to death before he could get either of the doors open.

'You've been staring at that page for ten minutes,' said Alison. 'What's so interesting?'

'Oh, nothing. I was just thinking—'

'Come on,' she said. 'Let me see.'

She scanned the page, and for a few seconds Nick thought he might be able to deceive her about which story he'd been reading. Then her face went white, and Nick sensed that her shock at reading the report was even greater than his. To him it was a coincidence: unnerving but somehow unreal, a story like thousands of others he'd read – and written. But to her it seemed – at least for a few seconds – like something more.

'He's not a relative, is he?'

'He's someone's,' said Nick, 'but not mine.'

The callousness of that remark appalled him. He was used to thinking of the human race simply as a source of copy. Now he was going to have to get used to being part of it.

'That didn't sound good,' he said. 'But it's not every day you read about yourself being struck by lightning.'

'Only it wasn't you,' Alison reminded him.

'No,' said Nick. 'But you know what I mean.'

'I think so,' Alison said.

'Nasty way to go,' said Nick.

'Very.'

They studied each other across the table. Then Alison said, 'You're hiding something.'

'No I'm not.'

'Yes, you are.' There was a long silence. 'Your birthday.'

'Oh, that. I thought you'd forgotten.'

'I never forget about birthdays.'

'7 April.'

'Aries,' she replied without hesitation.

'If you say so.'

She reached for the magazine in her bag. 'A typically Arian response.'

'I thought you said you didn't believe in astrology.'

'I don't. It's a mind drug for bored housewives and penniless students.' She paused. 'But that doesn't mean it isn't true.'

He opened his mouth and said 'I—' and stopped himself and went on, 'Once I picked up an old woman who wrote an astrology column. Sheila Starwoman. She told me she had fifty-two columns which she recycled every year in a different order. She'd been doing the same thing for thirty-five years.'

'I've read Sheila Starwoman,' she said dismissively. 'I can tell the future better than she can.' She opened the magazine and ran her finger down the page. 'Aries. Cryptic clues, abrupt reversals and enigmatic evasions. Don't even bother trying to make any sense out of your relationship right now.' She studied his face, and for an instant Nick had the feeling that she was looking right into his soul, seeing all his reversals and evasions. 'What's your favourite movie?'

Nick looked surprised. 'What has that got to do with anything?'

'You can tell a lot about a person by knowing their favourite movie.'

'It depends,' said Nick.

'On what?'

'What mood I'm in. Who I'm with. Whether I've got the screening times right.'

'What would you think if I told you mine was *Love Story*?'

'I'd think you needed help.'

'Actually it's *Thelma and Louise*.'

'All right. Mine is—'

'Stop!' She held up her hand. 'If it's *Rambo*, I don't want to know.'

'Do I look like the sort of person whose favourite movie would be *Rambo*?'

'Looks can be deceiving. Surely you'd know that—' she paused, 'as a taxi driver.'

Nick thought for a while before answering. '*The Maltese Falcon*,' he said. 'Humphrey Bogart. It's black and white.'

'"This is genuine coin of the realm, sir. With a dollar of this you can buy fifty dollars of talk." It's one of my favourites too.'

'You've got a good memory.'

'It was on cable the other night.'

'Cable is something else I don't have.'

She looked at him thoughtfully. 'No cable. No washing machine. No hair. Your life seems to be full of absences.'

'I've told you my favourite movie,' said Nick. 'What does it say about me?'

'I don't know yet. It might just confirm what I suspect already.'

'Which is?'

'Wait and see.'

The red car, a 1986 Alfa Romeo Alfetta, was still there, gleaming on its aluminium dais, and Nick had to admit it was the best-looking car in the yard. But it was an Alfetta, and Nick knew something about Alfettas, having been nearly bankrupted by one in his early twenties. Nearly ten years later his memory of owning an Alfetta (like most owners, he remembered owning rather than driving it) had been reduced to a kind of symbolic essence: window rubbers. Replacing them had been one of his first acts – courtesy of a tip from his then-girlfriend's older brother. At numbing cost Nick had had all the seals replaced – but the windows still leaked. Once, after driving back from Wollongong in a downpour, he'd found half an inch of water sloshing around beneath his seat. After that he avoided driving in the rain. It wasn't just his Alfetta, he soon realised, that took in water. It was *all* Alfettas. You never saw an Alfetta driving in the rain: you saw them lurking under bridges or loitering, like flashers, in underground carparks. He thought of this as he walked slowly around the dais, searching for evidence of the structural rust he knew must be hiding beneath the expensive re-spray.

'What do you think?' asked Alison.

'I like the colour.'

'Is that all you like?'

'It's Italian.'

'And?'

'It's probably older than you're looking for.'

Alison stroked a wing panel. 'It looks brand new.'

'It's had a brand new re-spray.'

'Isn't that a good thing?'

Nick didn't want to sound like a know-all, especially as she so obviously liked the car. Nor did he want to admit having owned one. That was Carmody's car, not his. On the other hand he liked her. You didn't stand by and let a woman you liked throw her money away on a second-hand Alfa. He crouched down to inspect the wheel arches. 'You know Italian means rust.'

'I thought Italian meant style.'

'It means rusting with style.'

'My Fiat never rusted.'

'If you say so.'

'So you're telling me not to buy it?'

'It's your money but . . . I'd urge you to consider something else.'

'You just object to the colour.'

'The colour's great. It's the car I object to.' He glanced around the yard. 'There's a Corolla over there. Nobody has a bad word to say about them.'

'I hate white cars.'

'What about that silver Lancer in the corner?'

'It's got those spoiler things on the back.'

A tall salesman in a blue suit was walking towards them. Alison pointed to a white Mazda 323 hatch. 'Let's look at that one.'

The salesman did his best to guide Alison back to the Alfetta until a casual question from Nick about window seals convinced him he was wasting his time.

She put a deposit on the Mazda with her credit card. As they walked out of the car yard Nick could feel his heart beating faster at the thought of where they might go next, and what they might do. Alison seemed to sense what was going through his mind. 'Well?' she said.

'I could buy you a drink,' said Nick. 'Since you're not driving home.'

'You could,' replied Alison. 'Or we could go back to my place and open a bottle of wine.'

The house in Drummond Street was a small red-brick two-storey terrace. The Italian restaurant next door had a banner that said 'Pizza-a-metro' – pizza by the metre. Between the house and restaurant was a cobbled alley that ended in an L-shaped garden where lupins and marrow plants were fighting a war of attrition against a shin-high sea of grass. 'I'm not sure why I'm showing you the garden,' said Alison. 'I'm not much of a gardener.'

'Nice house,' said Nick. 'How long have you had it?'

'It's not mine. I wish it was. I'm just renting.'

She shut the back door and locked it and hung the brass key on a hook beside the fridge. 'You're probably wondering about the front room.'

'It had crossed my mind,' said Nick, who'd been thinking of nothing else since they entered the house. The sight of a pair of men's runners and a milk crate full of dirty laundry had almost made his heart jump through his ribs.

'My flatmate, Corby. He owns the house. Or maybe his parents own it. I've never got to the bottom of the story.'

Nick tried hard but unsuccessfully to hide his disappointment.

'You don't have to worry about Corby. He's nocturnal. We only run into each other at weekends. You might find him a bit odd . . . Actually, he is a bit odd. But it's his house and he always cleans the bathroom, so I can't complain.'

Nick felt a sudden jolt. He remembered the morning in Hyde Park with Jess, the weedy-looking man asking him questions about bathroom scourers, the way he'd stood there making himself out to be a household cleaning fanatic. How could Alison possibly have known about that? Answer: she couldn't. Nick was imagining a connection where none existed. Or was he? He couldn't help sensing a curiosity in the way Alison looked at him that went beyond a simple interest in getting to know him.

She opened the fridge and took out a bottle of wine and handed it to Nick. While he opened the bottle she rummaged in the cupboards for glasses. She didn't seem to know where they were or even – it struck Nick – where they *might* be. She opened another cupboard and there, on the top shelf, stood half a dozen wine glasses.

Nick couldn't help noticing – and noticing her noticing – the film of ancient dust on the glasses, as if they hadn't been used for a very long time.

'They're not the ones I was looking for,' she said, 'but they'll do.'

They didn't go to bed that afternoon, although afterwards Nick had the feeling they could have done, if they'd opened another bottle of wine.

Some women liked to get sex out of the way early – some of Carolyn's legal colleagues, for instance (although not Carolyn). It was an experiment in compatibility, they used to say, between orbits of grim-faced cocktail waiters at the firm's Christmas party. It took the pressure off. To Nick, the counterargument seemed equally strong: it put the pressure on, to repeat the experiment.

There was something about Alison that mystified him. She had a way of looking at him sometimes that made him wonder if they hadn't met before, and she was waiting patiently for him to remember. And yet faces had always stuck in his mind – especially faces like hers. If they had met before, he was sure he would have remembered it.

She invited him to dinner the following Monday. By the sound of it, Corby was going to be there, and Nick made a half-hearted attempt to switch the venue – to his place in Coburg. But his cooking had never been more than utilitarian, often not even that, and in any case Alison had insisted. When he arrived at the house in Drummond Street, Nick found she was alone.

She had made spaghetti marinara, preceded by thick artichoke soup. He said little while they ate the soup: a reticence that Alison immediately attributed to his dislike of artichokes.

'Not true,' he replied.

TOM GILLING

'You can't fool me,' she said. 'Artichokes are a window to the soul. Every cook knows that.'

'All right,' said Nick. 'I'll admit they're not my favourite. But that doesn't mean I'm not open to conversion.'

She moved to take it away but he wouldn't let her. 'I've always thought I would like artichokes if only I could find the right person to cook them. I've got a feeling you might be the person.'

'Careful,' she said. 'I might think you were making assumptions.'

She asked him about his parents and he repeated the tale he'd told Homolka. It had become a sort of game he played with himself – the challenge to constantly refresh this imaginary past without making a mistake. He heard himself telling Alison the same spurious family history but this time the voice didn't sound like his. It sounded like the voice of an actor too tired to put any life into the lines he was reading. It occurred to Nick that it wasn't the future that was going to catch him out, but the past: the real past, in which he'd allowed himself to be bribed by Danny's father, or the imaginary past. Or both.

'I get the feeling you weren't very close,' was all Alison said, as if she knew something was missing from the story.

'Let's say we had our disagreements.'

Her own history, at least to begin with, seemed thoroughly conventional: she was the only child of an Adelaide general practitioner and the nurse who became his wife. Private school, then a semester at university, followed by eighteen months spent backpacking around Europe and South-East Asia, and finally a job as a flight attendant with Qantas. The only

163

unconventional aspect concerned her father, who – at the age of sixty-four – had abruptly divorced Alison's mother, citing irreconcilable differences of which she was apparently unaware, in order to take up with his twenty-six-year-old receptionist.

Two family histories without – as far as Nick could see – a single element in common, and yet somehow those two histories had brought them together, here in this musty dining room, across a candlelit table, over a meal of artichoke soup and spaghetti marinara.

'Did you know her?' Nick asked.

'Who?'

'The flirty receptionist. Your stepmother.'

'Did I say she was flirty? If you want my opinion he's more likely the one to blame. Mum certainly thinks so.'

'But you've met her?'

Alison stood up to collect the empty bowls while Nick swept the mussel shells onto a side plate and followed her into the kitchen. 'No. I think she's avoiding me. Although maybe she thinks I'm avoiding her. You realise she's younger than me? I just can't think of what I'd say to her. What we'd say to each other.'

Nick opened the fridge for the second of the two bottles he'd brought with him. 'I'm guessing we could manage another?'

'Why not? Since we're getting along so well.'

He unscrewed the lid of a Yarra Valley chardonnay. 'Would it be reckless of me to say I'm very glad our cars collided?'

'Probably,' she said.

She had a single bed, with a brightly coloured African bedspread, wedged between a varnished plywood wardrobe and a dressing table with an oval mirror. There was a nice but slightly shabby crimson Persian rug on the polished Baltic floorboards. The room was neat but seemed in some odd way temporary (there were no pictures on the walls, no photographs on the dressing table) – not the sort of room Nick would have predicted for a thirty-three-year-old woman with a well-paying airline job. Not that his own bedroom gave any more impression of permanence.

'You can always sleep on the floor,' she said, 'if you're worried there won't be room.'

'The less room the better,' said Nick.

She was pulling back the bedspread. He couldn't remember the last time he'd shared a single bed – not since he was a teenager, probably. He put his arms around her and bent down to kiss her ear. She shivered and pulled away.

'Careful. My ears are very sensitive.' She reached behind his shoulders and drew him down with both hands. Her voice fell to a whisper. 'Amazing things have happened to men who start kissing my ears.'

It was only a little story, half a dozen paragraphs beside a discount wine ad, but when Nick turned the page his eye went straight to it. The headline said, BIG DRY LOOKS CROOK FOR CRIMS.

Victorian criminals must be praying for rain to end the State's long drought as police revealed yesterday that dumped firearms were being uncovered at the bottoms of drying dams, lakes and creeks.

Victoria Police said weapons so far uncovered included a sawn-off .22 semi-automatic rifle and a bolt-action 12 gauge shotgun.

165

Checks were being carried out to see whether any of the guns could be linked to unsolved crimes. One rifle has been linked to a 20-year-old burglary and its original owner traced.

Senior Sergeant Frank Hare from Ballarat in western Victoria said four guns had been uncovered from the now-empty Lake Wendouree and at nearby Creswick. He said guns might have been dumped in lakes and dams after some categories were made illegal under new gun laws.

A number of dumped firearms had been found by people fossicking through rubbish exposed for the first time in decades on the beds of drying lakes and dams.

A week ago children playing on the banks of the Avoca River near Charlton discovered a dismantled lever-action .22 rifle wrapped in oilcloth which had been embedded in the mud. Forensic tests have linked this weapon to the unsolved shooting four years ago of a known drug dealer on Sydney's northern beaches, not far from the historic Barrenjoey lighthouse. Last year a World War II plane that ditched near Colac 55 years ago was found in Lake Corangamite.

Nick was sitting in a crowded cafe in Lygon Street but the world around him fell eerily quiet, as if for a few moments he was trapped inside his own noise-proof bubble. The urgent crackle of animated conversation sounded like a distant roar, a slowed-down tape-recording, or like voices heard underwater. He remembered the shooting near Barrenjoey lighthouse. He'd even gone up there with a photographer. The body had been removed but he'd seen the chalk marks indicating where the dead man had fallen.

The dealer was in his fifties, Nick recalled – a Russian, or at least someone from one of the former republics of the Soviet Union. To the police – and to most readers of the *Daily Star* – they were all Russians, just as any criminal of South-East Asian appearance was Vietnamese.

Detectives investigating the case had worked on the premise that he'd been murdered by a rival, or as punishment for an unpaid debt. He'd died from a single shot to the head: a good shot or a lucky shot, nobody could say which. The killer had left the ejected shell case on the ground.

Now, thanks to Nick, the gun had been recovered. And whatever the police knew, Nick knew that Chambers was not the harmless weekend pig-shooter he had wanted to believe. One thing Nick had learnt as crime reporter was that jumping to conclusions was as foolish as shutting your eyes to the obvious. The rifle he'd found in the tyre well of Chambers' panel van had been linked to the murder of a Sydney drug dealer. That didn't mean Chambers had any knowledge of what the gun had been used for, still less that he had used the gun to kill the dealer. Nevertheless, it established a connection – and connections, Nick knew, had a habit of spreading. Was there one between the Kevin Chambers who kept a gun hidden in the tyre well of his panel van and the Kevin Chambers who'd burnt to death in his ute? Or was it just one of those coincidences that made the world go round?

Once upon a time he would have been able to answer that himself. He would have known who to call, what questions to ask, and whether or not to believe the answers. Nick Carmody could have rung one of his former contacts at Police Headquarters to find out if there was anything about the rifle dumped in the Avoca River that hadn't been reported. But he wasn't Nick Carmody.

He wished he'd chosen somewhere else to dispose of the gun. He'd thought he was being clever but the truth was he'd panicked, and the land always found ways of punishing those who panicked.

'Flemington. Racecourse Road.'

The passenger looked vaguely familiar, as business travellers for some reason tended to. There was every chance Nick had picked him up before. He'd been drinking, either on the plane or in the business-class lounge before boarding. The smell of beer and whisky and stale cigarette smoke rolled off him.

The taxi gods had a habit of delivering Nick to the rank at Tullamarine Airport just in time to meet the last Qantas flight from Sydney – the only flight, as far as Nick could tell, that actually honoured the promise of unlimited free alcohol.

The man in the passenger seat had been staring at Nick intermittently from the moment he got in. He was staring at him again now.

Nick had learnt not to initiate conversations with passengers who showed no interest in talking. If they didn't talk it was usually because they had a reason for not talking. Twelve years at the *Daily Star*, interrogating and ingratiating himself with strangers, had given Nick a reasonable knowledge of human nature. But what he'd learnt behind a reporter's notebook paled next to what he was discovering behind the steering wheel of a taxi.

He'd envisaged taxi driving as a form of drudgery – a

dispiriting combination of bad pay, long hours, physical risk and enforced subservience to surly, ungracious, preoccupied strangers. And he was right. But it was also something else. A taxi, especially in the early hours of the morning, rattling along empty streets through comatose suburbs, was like a confessional without the screen. Ordinary people confessed extraordinary things, secure in their own anonymity.

Nick had expected to be bored but he was anything but. The money wasn't great but for some reason he didn't mind that. He'd tried once to buy the future. For now he was content to live in the present, where having enough to pay the bills was all that mattered.

Pretending to adjust his rear-vision mirror, Nick glanced sideways at the figure slumped in the passenger seat. He was a big man. He looked about forty. His right earlobe, the one Nick could see in the orange glow of the freeway lights, was ragged like a cat's, as if someone had taken a bite out of it. He wore a dark grey pinstripe suit that would have looked more stylish if it hadn't been a couple of sizes too small.

'Carmody,' he said at last. 'Nick Carmody.' It was a statement, not a question.

Nick didn't say anything.

'Come on, Carmody. You're not fooling me. I've read all about you.'

Nick was trapped and he knew it. Somewhere in the back of his mind he'd been anticipating this moment, even while he assured himself that it would never happen.

'Stackpole,' the man said. 'Ian Stackpole.'

Ian Stackpole. They had been at St Dominic's together but Stackpole was four years older. His father, Lawrie, was a racehorse trainer who'd trained a filly that ran third in the Melbourne Cup. Ian was a useful rugby player and played a few games for one of the Sydney clubs while he was still at school. Then his father suffered a stroke and the stables were sold. In his last year Stackpole was made a school prefect. One afternoon he'd busted Nick and Danny Grogan for smoking. He must have flunked his final exams because after leaving St Dominic's he went straight into the police. Nick remembered running into him at a coronial inquest into the death of an Aboriginal youth, standing sheepishly in the lobby of the Glebe Coroner's Court, dying for a cigarette but not daring to go outside in case he missed his call. Stackpole hadn't recognised Nick in his cheap reporter's suit but Nick had introduced himself. If he hadn't then maybe Stackpole would not have recognised him now.

'Ian,' he said, trying to sound calm. 'You look different.'

'Like fuck.'

For a few seconds neither spoke. Then Stackpole broke the silence. 'What the hell,' he said in a more conciliatory voice. 'Maybe I do. I try not to look in the mirror too much these days.'

'You look all right,' said Nick.

'I wish I felt all right. I can't piss and my balls are turning blue. Other than that I'm a picture of health.' He stared at Nick. 'So what's the story – or am I going to have to invent one? I mean, that's what you blokes do, isn't it? Ask a couple of questions and then make up the rest.' Ignoring the 'No Smoking' sticker on the dashboard, he fumbled in his pocket for a cigarette. 'Mate, I'm sorry. I almost forgot. This is your private pain and humiliation we're talking about. You don't

170

want a stranger like me sticking my nose into it.' He found a cigarette and stuck it in his mouth and said through pursed lips, 'Coroner's inquiry, wasn't it? You were working for the *Star*. Just started, I seem to remember. But pretty full of yourself all the same.' He gazed around Homolka's battered taxi. 'Felt like a change of career, did you?'

'Something like that.'

'No, mate. I'm interested. *Star* reporter goes missing. Quite a story. They found your car somewhere. I'm trying to remember the place . . . Somewhere down south, wasn't it?'

Nick realised that holding out now was pointless. He would have to go along with Stackpole and see where it took him. 'Seven Mile Beach.'

'Seven Mile Beach. That's it.' Stackpole made several feckless attempts to light his cigarette before Nick passed him the dashboard lighter. 'Thought you might have drowned, didn't they? I knew that was bullshit. At fucking St Dominic's they didn't teach us much but at least they taught us to swim. You remember the outdoor pool? And that sadist McCluskey. "Who's going to break the ice for us today?" Shove. I heard that bastard had a stroke.'

Nick shrugged. 'I wouldn't know, Ian. I haven't really kept in contact since I left.'

'No,' said Stackpole. 'I don't suppose you have.' He blew smoke over his shoulder. 'So here I am, mate. A passenger in your taxi. Are you going to tell me what happened or what?'

'It's a long story,' said Nick. 'I'll tell you all about it one day.'

'I bet you will.' Stackpole sucked on his cigarette. 'Of course, I could just ring up the papers. I guess they'd know what to do with a yarn like this. What do you reckon?'

Nick didn't answer.

'Maybe I'll just sit on it for a bit,' said Stackpole. 'See if I can come up with a better idea. I might even have a go at writing it myself. Special correspondent. Do you think they'd come at that?'

He flicked his ash into the ashtray and stared for a long time out of the side window. When he turned around his expression had changed. Nick knew he had to keep him talking.

'What about you, Ian?'

'What about me?'

'Are you still in the force?'

'No, mate. I'm not.'

'Been out of it long?'

'Not long enough.'

Constable Ian Stackpole's career had been effectively over from the moment he testified in court about the death of an Aboriginal man in custody. According to the custody sergeant the man had fallen awkwardly while being escorted to his cell. Aboriginal men had a habit of falling while being escorted to their cells. They fell and from time to time they didn't get up again. All Stackpole had to say was that, like his colleagues, he'd seen the prisoner throw a punch. But Stackpole wouldn't say it. He didn't say the punch wasn't thrown; just that he hadn't seen it. Not seeing that punch finished his career. The irony was the coroner took no notice of Stackpole's evidence and decided that 'reasonable force' had been used to subdue the prisoner. Another whitewash, and as far as most of the media were concerned, Constable Ian Stackpole was as complicit as all his mates. But to his mates he was a liability, a colleague who couldn't be counted on to say the right thing when it mattered. In those few minutes on the witness stand, Stackpole had fucked up his life, not by anything he'd said but by something he hadn't said. If he was bitter about the way things had turned out, Nick thought, he had every right to be.

'Family?' asked Nick.

'Ex-wife,' said Stackpole. 'Three ex-kids. I've just been in Sydney to see them. I hadn't laid eyes on them for six months. She gave me an hour.'

'Too bad.'

'You got any?'

'Kids? No.'

'Then you don't know what I'm talking about.'

Stackpole squinted at his watch but seemed unable to read the time. 'What time is it?'

'Just after eleven.'

They drove in silence for the rest of the journey. A steady drizzle was falling. Once or twice Stackpole appeared to nod off, only to wake up abruptly as his head lurched forwards. By the time they reached Racecourse Road he was in one of his wide-awake phases. 'Come in,' he said. 'I'll make some coffee.'

He spoke as if both of them needed sobering up.

'I'm supposed to be working,' said Nick.

'Then don't come in.'

Stackpole clambered unsteadily out of the seat and held onto the door for balance. Nick switched off the engine.

Stackpole slammed the door and began stumbling towards the gate. He lived in one half of a dilapidated pair of semis. His half was the more dilapidated. A downpipe had come away from the gutter and stood out from the wall like some crazy flagpole. Letters were spilling out of the mailbox, as though it hadn't been cleared for weeks. Nick removed his takings and took his ID card from its holder and locked the taxi. Then he followed Stackpole up the broken cement path to the front door. As he climbed the steps, the older man suddenly tripped, almost hitting his head against a brick pillar. Nick didn't say anything but as he helped him to his feet a monstrous thought flashed through his mind. If Stackpole had fallen and split his head on the pillar, the problem of what to do about him would have been solved. From the way he'd described his life, who would have missed him? The thought seemed to belong not to him – that is, to the person he recognised as himself – but to a stranger he didn't know. He felt Stackpole push him away – out of embarrassment, or because he knew what Nick was thinking?

'Fucking steps,' said Stackpole.

He held up the brass key and prodded clumsily at the lock until the teeth of the key disappeared and the door opened. Groping along the wall, Stackpole switched on the light. Nick shut the door behind him.

The carpet was orange shagpile. Overflowing ashtrays and unwashed plates lay everywhere. The house smelt of beer. Around the walls were piles of form guides, circled and scribbled on with red ballpoint, each held in place by a brick. Nick sat on the sofa while Stackpole crashed around the kitchen in search of coffee.

When he finally emerged it wasn't mugs of coffee he was carrying but a bottle of Famous Grouse. He put down the whisky and stood there swaying for a few moments, as though trying to remember why there was someone else in the house. Then he sat down heavily in the scruffier of a pair of armchairs.

He pointed vaguely at a bow-fronted sideboard in the corner of the room. 'You'll find a glass in there.'

His own glass was on the floor. He picked it up and unscrewed the Famous Grouse and poured himself a triple. Then he shook a cigarette out of a crumpled packet of Silk Cut and bent his head towards it – like a donkey groping for a piece of apple.

Nick said, 'You still follow the horses.'

Stackpole didn't answer at once. As he focused his gaze, it seemed to Nick that he'd forgotten who he was talking to.

'I should do,' he said at last. 'That's how I earn a living.'

'You're a trainer.'

Stackpole tapped his ash into a heavy glass ashtray. 'I'm a bookie.'

Nick thought at first he was joking. Ex-policemen haunted bookies – they didn't become bookies.

Stackpole picked up his drink. 'You don't believe me?'

'I believe you.'

'The old man was a trainer. Had a horse that ran third in the Melbourne Cup. Did you know that?'

Nick tried hard to look impressed. He remembered being impressed once, a long time ago. But now it didn't seem that impressive.

'I do all right,' Stackpole replied, to a question that hadn't been asked. Then he stood up and said, 'I need a piss.'

Nick gazed at the walls of the living room, which were hung with photographs of Stackpole's life. There was a picture of him with his father at Randwick racecourse; another of him at his passing out parade at Goulburn Police College; another with three boys (his sons, maybe?) building a sandcastle in front of Bondi pavilion. He reached for a scrapbook lying on a shelf below the coffee table. Pasted inside were newspaper photographs of Lawrie Stackpole's third-placed filly, of Ian as captain of St Dominic's Second XI and caked in mud with his team-mates from Eastwood Rugby Club. And cuttings: from *Australian Horse Racing*, *Horse Racing News* and the *Winning Post*; from the *Australian Police Gazette* (a picture of a police cadet fainting on parade under the headline NEW RECRUIT PASSES OUT IN STYLE) and the *Daily Star*.

As he sat there, flicking through the pages of Stackpole's scrapbook, Nick thought about his own life, which existed in a kind of vacuum, a present cut loose from the past. He hadn't kept a single photograph, a single postcard or newspaper cutting to remind him of the person he had once been. He was beginning to wonder whether that person had ever existed. If he could invent one life then why shouldn't he have invented two? And yet there it was – his byline – on page three of the *Daily Star*, above a half-page report of the coronial inquiry that spelt the end of Stackpole's police career. Seeing that byline filled Nick with a sense of uncertainty, of not knowing who or what he was. Of being somebody pretending to be nobody – or nobody pretending to be somebody.

Stackpole shuffled back into the room and sat down. His cigarette had gone out in his absence and it took him three attempts to re-light it. He finished the triple Scotch he'd poured himself and reached for the bottle and poured another. They stared at each other in silence. It seemed to Nick that all he had to do was keep Stackpole drinking and sooner or later he would simply fall asleep. With a hangover like that, Nick thought, he wasn't going to remember much of the previous night.

*   *   *

It was lying on the doorstep when he got home: a glossy envelope with the words, 'Congratulations, Kevin Chambers!' emblazoned in red across the top left-hand corner.

Rather than stuffing everything in the rusty mailbox, as he was paid to do, as he did on every other day, the postie had made a special trip from the gate to leave the envelope on the porch, where it would be safe from the weather.

Nick unlocked the front door and took the letter inside and dropped it on the kitchen table while he boiled the kettle. It was 3.46 a.m. and he'd earned precisely $106.90, after expenses, for driving twelve hours in the rain. In light of these facts the words 'Congratulations, Kevin Chambers!' had a sarcastic ring.

He put a tea bag in the mug and poured the water. As he sniffed the milk, he drew back in disgust. Then he opened the envelope. The letter said:

Dear Kevin Chambers,

Have you ever wondered where you came from? Who your ancestors were? What happened to those long lost cousins?

All this information can be yours if you subscribe to the WORLD BOOK OF CHAMBERS! Accept our invitation to subscribe to the WORLD BOOK OF CHAMBERS and be amazed at how many CHAMBERS there are around the globe.

Subscribe now to the WORLD BOOK OF CHAMBERS and you will receive a 50% discount to the normal price of $49.95 PLUS free postage PLUS a bonus copy ABSOLUTELY FREE.

To guarantee your own inclusion in the WORLD BOOK OF CHAMBERS please complete the enclosed questionnaire and return it together with your cheque or postal order for $49.95.

This is a UNIQUE OPPORTUNITY to see your name in print so DO NOT DELAY. The WORLD BOOK OF CHAMBERS will not be sold through book stores. Subscribe NOW to avoid disappointment.

Nick thought about how his world had shrunk. The big picture no longer seemed important. It was the small picture that was starting to keep him awake at night. His universe was shrinking, in time and space. Each week it got a little smaller. Once there had been thousands of names, then hundreds, and soon there would only be one: Chambers. He tore up the letter and threw away the pieces.

'So this is the dog I've heard so much about?'

It was a rhetorical question but something about the way she said it made Nick feel he ought to answer. He'd noticed it before, the way she fished for information without actually asking for it. Justifiable curiosity was how he'd explained it to himself: after all they had only known each other for a few weeks and this was Alison's first visit to De Carle Street.

'She's a greyhound, isn't she?'

'A superannuated greyhound, yes.'

'I thought greyhounds were stupid dogs but she looks quite . . . '

'What?'

'Intelligent. Crafty.'

'You can tell that just by looking, can you?'

'Of course. Can't you?'

'Not in a dog.'

'But we were talking about dogs, weren't we?'

Nick opened the door and stood aside as the excited dog hurled itself through the gap.

'Careful,' said Nick. 'She gets a bit slobbery sometimes.'

'How long have you had her?'

'Not long.' He stood there, half doubled-over, while the greyhound nuzzled his groin. 'She'd be able to give you the exact date. If she could talk.' He tried to push the animal away but the wet nose and slippery tongue kept squirming past his hands.

'She's very affectionate,' said Alison, crouching beside her. 'I like a dog that's affectionate. What's her name?'

'You won't believe this. Actually it's Fred.'

'Daring,' said Alison. 'Original. I'd ask why . . . but on second thoughts I think I'll leave it a mystery.' She stood up. 'So, can I ask what you're cooking?'

'It's not so much what I *am* cooking,' said Nick, attempting to push the animal back outside, 'as what I *was* cooking before the power went.'

Alison glanced at the illuminated light above her head.

'It's back now,' said Nick, 'but the meat won't be done, and I'd rather not serve it raw.' He shrugged apologetically. 'Do you mind if we go out instead?'

They went to a Vietnamese restaurant Nick had driven past many times in his taxi. He'd read a review in the *Age* that gave it fourteen points out of twenty – which was as good a score as anyone ever got from the *Age*'s restaurant reviewer. On each occasion Nick had looked at the restaurant it had been full – there was sometimes even a queue on the pavement outside

– but this evening only three tables were taken. A bored teenage waitress was folding napkins on the counter.

'I thought you said this restaurant would be crowded,' said Alison.

'It usually is. We can go somewhere else if you prefer.'

'You've made me curious. And I've never eaten Vietnamese.'

'Really?' Nick was surprised. He assumed that in the course of a few years an airline flight attendant would have been everywhere and eaten everything.

'You'd be amazed,' said Alison. 'Some of the most unadventurous travellers I know spend their entire working lives on planes.'

Nick was becoming used to her exaggerations but still found it hard to pick when she was pulling his leg. 'There's a Thai place down the road,' he said. 'It's supposed to be all right.'

'Bored with Thai,' Alison said decisively. 'Let's eat here.'

The food wasn't bad but somehow it wasn't as good as he'd hoped. Visiting a restaurant after reading a glowing review was, in Nick's experience, always a rather dispiriting exercise. Either the food was as good as the reviewer had said and the whole city was fighting for a table, or it wasn't and you sat there feeling deceived. In any case, it was more enjoyable to stumble upon a place that was still undiscovered. Still, the bill was reasonable and the teenage waitress, once she'd stopped folding napkins, was very attentive and Alison was effusive about the crab and white fungus soup, so the evening was a success despite the unpromising start.

At some level Nick couldn't quite bring himself to believe that things had turned out the way they had. He'd never believed in love at first sight: in almost every relationship he'd known, persuasion had played as much of a part as attraction. Neither he nor Alison had taken much persuading. For all their enjoyment of one another's company, he couldn't help feeling that there was a lot they were not telling each other. He thought of how long he and Carolyn had known each other – only to discover at the bitter end that they were complete strangers. Time, he'd found out, was no guarantee of wisdom or compatibility. Perhaps that's why he felt so happy with Alison: because time didn't enter into it. The past and the future both fell away. He wondered how long it could last – that sense of living only in the present.

'. . . or then again, maybe not,' said Alison.

'Not what?'

'Have you been listening, or have I been talking to myself for the last five minutes?'

'Sorry,' said Nick, reaching across to touch her hand. 'I just remembered something I had to do.'

'And what was that?'

'One of the indicator lights has blown. I meant to leave Homolka a note to get it replaced.'

Alison poured the last of the wine into her glass. 'I'm glad my conversation stimulates such profound reflections.'

'Someone nearly ran into the back of me last night because he couldn't see I was turning right. I don't fancy it happening again.'

He was staring at the little gold ingot she wore on a chain around her neck. It was the first time he'd really studied it. One face was plain but the ingot was hanging back to front and Nick could read the letters AMC engraved on the reverse.

'That's a nice pendant,' he said.

'Yes,' she answered brightly. 'It is.'

'What do the initials stand for?'

She looked down and immediately turned the ingot around. 'It belonged to my mother. Before she married my father.'

'It suits you,' he said.

'Really? And why do you say that?'

'Oh, I don't know. It's simple. Elegant. I like jewellery that's simple and elegant.'

'And that's me, is it? I like the sound of elegant. I'm not so sure about simple.'

The waitress got up to open the door while Alison added some coins to the tip Nick had been going to leave. As they stood on the pavement, Alison's mobile phone rang. She glanced at the caller ID before switching off the phone. 'It's Corby,' she said.

'Don't mind me.'

'I don't really feel like talking to Corby.'

It wasn't the first time Corby had rung while she and Nick had been out together.

'I think he might be trying to tell you something,' said Nick.

'Of course he's trying to tell me something. Otherwise he wouldn't be ringing. But whatever it is, I'm certain it can wait until tomorrow.'

'I get the impression Corby doesn't like me. Or doesn't like the thought of you liking me. One or the other.'

'Would it matter?'

'Not really,' said Nick.

'You're wrong anyway,' said Alison. 'I've never heard Corby say anything uncomplimentary about you. It's just his manner. He's an acquired taste.'

'And you've acquired it?'

'I wouldn't go that far. Let's just say I've had to deal with much worse than Corby. At least Corby doesn't have a buzzer he can press every time he wants my attention.'

Nick put both arms around her. Just for a second he felt her pull away, as if there was something she wanted to say before being kissed. As they crossed the road she drew his arm over her shoulders and hooked her fingers into the pocket of his jeans, an embrace that was part cuddle, part clasp, at the same time tender and anxiously possessive.

The job was supposed to be from Essendon to Tullamarine Airport. The pick-up was outside a block of units. No phone number. Passenger's name: Mick.

Hardly the choicest job, but the passenger had asked for him by name. That wasn't unusual. Unlike some drivers Nick did his best to keep up a conversation when it was offered, and if a passenger asked for a card, he was happy to give them one.

He knew he would spend ten minutes waiting on the street for the passenger to come out, and another half hour on the taxi rank at the other end. Nick never sat on a rank if he could help it, but once you'd been dragged out to the airport you didn't have much choice – unless you wanted to drive back empty.

Nick found the address in Essendon: a block of twenty-four sixties-style red-brick units. As he'd anticipated, the passenger was nowhere in sight. He sat outside for a while, periodically honking his horn, then radioed base for instructions. He assured the caller that he'd arrived at the address on time although the truth was he'd turned up a couple of minutes late. The radio caller told him to wait.

It was all about blame-shifting. An operator would prefer to leave a driver sitting idle for fifteen minutes than be accused of screwing up a booking. Nick waited. Five minutes passed and there was still no sign of the passenger. Nick was ready to give the job up as a no-show. By now the passenger was probably halfway down the Tullamarine Freeway – in some other bastard's taxi.

A middle-aged woman came out of the block of units. She was carrying a black bag that could conceivably have been described as luggage. She stared at him as she walked past. Obviously she wasn't the passenger. Nick picked up the radio and made another call to base.

The caller sounded harassed, as usual. 'Driver ninety-two, is that you again?'

The pick-up address had already disappeared from the screen. Nick asked him to repeat it.

'Haven't you picked up yet?'

'I'm still waiting.'

'Have you used your horn?'

'Of course I've used my horn.'

'Don't be sarcastic with me, driver.' He repeated the address. He'd given Nick the passenger's name but Nick asked him to repeat that too.

'Carmody,' said the caller.

At first Nick thought he must have misheard. 'Say that again, please.'

'Carmody. Do you need me to spell that?'

For a moment Nick couldn't speak. He thought he was

going to be sick. Was this a joke – or was someone trying to frighten him?

'Driver, is there a problem?'

Nick looked up at the building. The units facing the street all had balconies. He could see pot plants trailing from some, stacks of plastic chairs, the outline of bicycles and drying racks and surfboards. Was someone up there watching him?

'I asked you a question, driver.'

'No,' Nick managed to answer. 'No problem.'

Carmody was a common enough surname, Nick told himself as he dialled the number for directory inquiries. He was sitting in the carpark of a drive-in McDonald's. The voice computer asked him for a name.

'Carmody,' he said. He spelt it out – 'C-A-R-M-O-D-Y' – and repeated the pick-up address.

The voice recognition computer couldn't recognise his voice. Computers could never recognise his voice. After a few seconds a human operator came on the line. Nick repeated the name and address.

'Nothing for Carmody,' said the operator. 'Are you sure you have the right address?'

Nick hung up without answering. He hadn't expected anyone called Carmody to be listed at that address. He put away his mobile phone and stared at the customers queuing inside McDonald's. On a different night he might have been one of them – staring up at the illuminated menu and wondering whether to have large or small fries with his Big Mac. He didn't know what was going on but he knew that something was. He thought about his life, about the choices he'd made that had brought him to this point, the decisions that had propelled him in this direction rather than another. Somebody was trying to make him pay for those decisions – but who?

He tried to think of all the people who had an interest in finding Nick Carmody. There was Harry Grogan, of course. He would know that Nick had disappeared. As far as Nick was concerned, the business between them was over. It had been over the moment the final cheque had arrived. But perhaps Grogan didn't see it that way. To Harry Grogan, Nick might have felt like a loose end that needed tying off. Nick knew things, and knowledge like that could be dangerous for a man like Grogan. He'd been Danny's friend, maybe his only friend, but Grogan wasn't the sentimental kind.

Then there was Michael Flynn. If he'd been Flynn, he would have made finding Nick Carmody his number-one priority. Tracking down the fugitive hit-and-run driver would have made his career. But Flynn wouldn't have known where to start looking, unless . . . Suddenly he remembered Stackpole. Of course it had to be Stackpole. He tried to remember everything they had spoken about in the taxi, and later in the living room in Racecourse Road. Stackpole had nothing personal to gain from turning Nick in. It would have been enough for him to let Nick know that he could if he wanted to.

Two bikers in black leathers and storm-trooper boots drove their Harley Davidsons into the carpark, took their Nazi helmets off and waddled inside to join the queue. Maybe it *had* been a coincidence – not every phone user had a listed number. Carmody could have been the name of a visitor, or a tenant. Maybe he was imagining a threat where none existed.

Maybe Stackpole was just trying to put the wind up him. Maybe.

'He's not here,' a woman's voice called out from behind the sagging timber fence.

Nick hadn't realised he was being watched. He looked around.

'I said he's not here.' The speaker paused. 'Who are you looking for?'

'Mr Stackpole,' said Nick, walking towards the gap in the fence through which the woman had been spying on him.

She was wearing a nylon apron and pink slippers and her grey hair was in a net. 'You won't find him,' she said. 'Are you the police?'

'No. I'm a friend.'

'The police were here the other day. I seen them come. He wasn't in then either.'

'Can you tell me where he is?'

'They took him away. Last night.'

'Took him away – who did?'

'The ambos. Took him away on a stretcher.' She pointed to an upstairs window. 'I saw it out of that window there. Plastic mask and everything. I thought he must be dead.' She hesitated. 'You should see the bottles he puts out every week.'

'Do you know where they took him?'

'Hospital. I don't know which one. You'd have to ask. What are you – a friend of his?'

'Old friend,' said Nick.

'He's got a wife, you know. And kids. Never sees 'em, but.'

'I know.'

'They live up there.' She waved a thumb absentmindedly over her left shoulder. 'Sydney.'

'I know.'

'You know Sydney?'

'I know his wife and children live in Sydney.'

'Never been there,' the woman said. 'Never wanted to either. Here's good enough for me. Too old to start again.'

'I've got to go,' said Nick.

'I told him he was ill. "See a doctor," I said, but he never would. Mine was the same. Cancer. They didn't even open him up. Too far gone, they said. Wasn't worth the trouble. I said to your friend, let them have a look. Get the doctors to take some x-rays. You never know what's growing inside you. But I don't think he wanted to know.' She tucked a stray wisp of grey hair back under the net. 'Tell him I'll bring in the mail. And tell him not to worry about the garden.'

Looking around him as he walked back to the gate, Nick doubted that Stackpole had ever worried about the garden.

Pretending to be a family friend, Nick rang around the city's hospitals until he found that a man named Ian Stackpole had been admitted late the previous night to the emergency ward at the Royal Melbourne Hospital. He thought about the time. It must have been just after Stackpole had called the taxi company with a hoax booking for Nick Carmody.

The nurse he spoke to wouldn't comment on his condition. Nick wondered whether he'd had a stroke. An overweight middle-aged male smoker who drank too much – Stackpole was the archetypal twenty-first-century stroke victim.

At the flower shop downstairs he bought a couple of

bunches of copper-coloured chrysanthemums. The thought crossed his mind that Stackpole's ex-wife might be there.

When the lift doors opened Nick's eye was drawn, as always, to the sight of his own shaven head. Even now, it could still take him by surprise. At a conscious level he identified fully with the image he saw in the mirror. But subconsciously he still half-expected to wake up and find his hair had grown back in the night.

He found the ward and walked around it, looking at the names on the doors. Eventually he spotted the name 'Stackpool' on a blue door at the far end of a corridor. He wasn't a grammatical pedant but the misspelt name offended him. He went back to the nurses' station and borrowed a pen and corrected the 'pool' to 'pole'. It wasn't strictly visiting time but no one seemed to be patrolling.

He stood outside for a few moments, watching Stackpole through the small square of wire-reinforced glass. There was no sign of his ex-wife or their children. A tray of food lay untouched on the table beside him. Stackpole was lying in bed staring out of the window.

'Well, well,' said Stackpole. 'Look what the cat dragged in.'

Nick looked around for a vase. Not finding one, he put the flowers in the sink.

It was a double room overlooking a small patch of lawn where two nurses sat on a bench, smoking. The other bed was empty.

'How did you know I was here?' Stackpole asked without looking around.

'Your neighbour saw the ambulance come.'

'I bet she did.'

'She asked me to tell you she'd bring in the mail.'

Stackpole nodded. 'She'll enjoy reading that.'

A silence followed. Then Nick asked, 'How are you feeling?'

'Like shit. If you're interested.'

Nick saw his face contort with pain. He was hooked up to various monitors. A thin plastic catheter disappeared under the bedclothes.

'Do they know what it is?'

'They reckon it's kidney stones.'

Nick had known people with kidney stones. They didn't look like this. He glanced down at the uneaten meal. 'Can I get you anything?'

'Apart from a new pair of kidneys, you mean?'

'If the food's no good I can buy you something from the canteen.'

'Thanks. But no thanks. If I need anything I'll get it myself.'

'What about your wife and the kids?'

'Ex-wife, ex-kids,' said Stackpole. 'Why are you here, Carmody? Don't tell me you're one of those hospital weirdos. The sort that likes visiting strangers and showing them the way to Jesus. Have you come to show me the way, Carmody, is that it?'

'I haven't come to show you the way to Jesus, Ian.'

'Then why have you come?'

'Somebody made a booking for a taxi last night. They asked for me personally. The passenger's name was Nick Carmody.'

'Very interesting. But what's it got to do with me?'

'Come on, Ian. I know it was you. It had to be. You decided it was payback time.'

'Payback? That's more your style, isn't it? The *Star* always enjoyed a bit of payback, didn't it?'

'This is not a joke.'

'It wasn't me, Carmody. I was at home. Writhing in agony. It might hurt you to hear this but last night you weren't uppermost in my thoughts. If you think someone's jerking you around you'll have to find another culprit.'

'Are you sure?'

'Am I sure of what – that I didn't book a taxi in your name? Yes, I think I'd remember that. Of course I haven't got an alibi, Carmody. You'll just have to take my word for it.'

Nick walked to the window. If Stackpole hadn't made the call, who had? He still didn't believe Flynn was capable of finding him. The police? There had been nothing in the Sydney papers about Nick Carmody being charged over the hit-and-run. Maybe the girl had confessed. If there was a warrant out for his arrest, he would have read about it. As far as the police were concerned, Carmody was just another name in a missing persons file – and as long as he didn't attempt to cash any of Harry Grogan's cheques, he'd stay that way.

Another possibility struck him: Kevin Chambers. *What if Chambers was the one jerking him around?* He'd become so comfortable with the thought of being Kevin Chambers that he'd almost forgotten Kevin Chambers already existed. Maybe Chambers had made the call.

Nick had the sense of being involved in a game in which the rules had abruptly changed. In some mysterious way their positions had been reversed and Chambers was pretending to be him.

There were dozens of ways Chambers could have tracked him to Melbourne. Nick knew that most fugitives gave themselves away the moment they needed money. Their first visit to an automatic teller machine was usually their last. But it wasn't only money that left a trail. Nick wished he'd destroyed Chambers' panel van but it was too late to worry about that now. If he was lucky it would have been reduced to a rack of spare parts, but luck wasn't something Nick felt he could count on. If it was Chambers who'd made the hoax call then Nick needed to know why, and what he might do next, and in order to answer that, he needed to know what kind of man Chambers was, what sort of life he lived, whether he'd ever been in trouble with the police. If Chambers did come looking for him he would start with the panel van, and the panel van would lead him to Melbourne.

He turned to look at Stackpole. 'I need some information.'

'Why would I want to help you, Carmody?'

'Because you know how to get it, and because I'm asking.'

Stackpole reached for a glass of water.

'That probably sounded more touching to you than it does to me. You come here accusing me of things and now you're begging me for help. Pardon me if I can't see what's in this for me.'

'Believe me,' said Nick, 'if I could ask anyone else, I would.'

Stackpole stared at him. For a moment Nick thought he was going to tell him to get out. He couldn't have blamed him; Nick's behaviour so far hadn't exactly been honourable. Stackpole scrunched up his face, as though enduring another spasm of pain. Then he asked, 'What sort of information?'

The trouble with working a double shift was that you were often too tired to drive the next day. If you were too tired you missed the good jobs that came in on the radio. You drove like a zombie. You misheard instructions and, out of sheer fatigue, you gave up searching for jobs on the street and took refuge on taxi ranks. In the end you took home forty dollars and might as well have spent the whole time in bed.

Nick got in at 3 a.m. and took the telephone off the hook. Alison was somewhere between Melbourne and Tokyo. He found her destination hard to remember. It was nearly one in the afternoon when he woke. He put the phone back on its cradle, and heard it ring straight away. He picked up the receiver.

'Carmody?'

He recognised Stackpole's voice.

'Yes.'

'Where have you been?'

'Asleep.'

'I've been ringing you all morning.'

'I left the phone off the hook.'

'Do you want that information or not?'

'Yes. Of course—'

'You'll have to come and get it. I'm not giving it to you over the phone.'

For the first time in months, it was pouring with rain. The temperature had dropped about ten degrees. The drought seemed to have broken while Nick was asleep.

He found Stackpole sitting up in bed. A tray of uneaten food was lying on the bedside table. The various tubes he'd been hooked up to last time appeared to have been removed. Nick shook his jacket in the sink and sat down.

'Feeling any better?' he asked.

'Not much.'

'When will they let you go home?'

'They won't. They're keeping me under observation.'

'So how long—'

Stackpole cut him off. 'Do you want to hear this or not?'

He opened the drawer of the bedside table and pulled out the scrap of paper on which Nick had written the registration number of Chambers' panel van. Nick waited for him to speak. He didn't want to know about the vehicle, of course. He wanted to know what the vehicle revealed about its owner.

'The registered owner of that vehicle is a woman,' said Stackpole. 'Alison Mary Lake. Previously Alison Mary Chambers. 16 Beach Street, Curl Curl.' He looked up. 'That's a Sydney address, in case you've forgotten.' He handed Nick the scrap of paper. 'No criminal record.'

Nick stared in disbelief at the name. Alison Mary Chambers. The name matched the initials on the ingot around her neck – the ingot she claimed to have been given by her mother. But they were her initials, or at least they had been until she changed her name. Alison had married a man called Lake and taken his name. But her maiden name was Chambers. She had to be Kevin Chambers' sister. Nick remembered the accident in Box Hill. The bus driver must have taken down his number. Someone had identified the owner and made a claim on the insurance company – and the letter had gone to Alison. For some reason she had come searching for him. But why?

The chain of connections started clanking through Nick's head. He and Alison hadn't met by chance at all. Chance had nothing to do with it. Somehow it was all down to Alison.

'What about Kevin Chambers?'

'What about him?'

'Does he have a record?'

'Juvenile stuff. Property damage, offensive language in a public place. Nothing since he was sixteen.' He paused. 'What were you expecting?'

'I don't know.'

Stackpole was manoeuvring himself out of bed.

'What are you doing?' Nick asked.

'What does it look like? I'm getting out of bed. I'm going down the corridor to have a piss. And after that I'm going home.'

'So you've been discharged?'

'I need a drink. I'm discharging myself.'

'You can't do that.'

'Watch me.'

'Don't be crazy, Ian. It's belting down out there. And you're wearing pyjamas. Have you got any clothes?'

'You might not believe it, but I wasn't thinking about what I was wearing when the ambos took me away. I thought I was dying. It didn't occur to me to pack. I'm lucky they put shoes on me.'

'Jesus, Ian – you can't walk out in pyjamas.'

'I wasn't planning to. I'll borrow some clothes on my way out. There'll be something lying about.' He noticed Nick's green jacket lying in the sink. 'I'll take this.'

'What am I supposed to do?'

'Stay here. Give me a head start. If anyone comes in say I've gone for a walk around the ward.'

It seemed like a mad idea to Nick – but the whole world suddenly seemed mad to Nick. The woman whose bed he shared wasn't the person he'd thought she was five minutes ago.

He stared out of the window. Rain was falling in sheets that dragged across the face of the building like the slow vanes of a waterwheel.

Between distant growls of thunder Nick could hear the sound of ambulances arriving and departing from casualty. He watched jagged forks of lightning quiver in the purple sky. He felt dead inside, as if he no longer existed.

After twenty minutes a nurse came in: a no-nonsense woman from the Pacific islands. She glanced at the empty bed and then at Nick. 'Where is the patient?'

Nick began to say what Stackpole had told him to say. Then he stopped. What was the point? Stackpole would be well away by now. In any case the nurse wasn't listening. She looked at Nick with a kind of weary contempt before walking out.

The hospital was a maze. Nick made several unsuccessful attempts to reach the main entrance before finding himself next to a door marked 'Emergency Exit'. There was a small terrace outside. Water cascaded from the awning. Beyond the terrace a covered walkway connected the L-shaped building he'd come from with an older building. Through the rain Nick could just make out a sign that said 'Way Out'. A broken black umbrella was lying in a metal bin next to the door and Nick took it.

A small crowd was standing around the ambulance in spite of the rain. Nick wondered what the ambulance was doing in the hospital carpark, rather than in the ambulance bay outside casualty. Its lights were flashing.

An empty taxi cruised by and he raised an arm but the taxi driver either didn't see him or had another job to go to. In weather like this there wasn't much point trying to make a phone booking because the switchboard would be jammed.

His best chance was to hail a taxi off the street but almost every taxi he saw was full and Nick knew he could be standing in the rain for an hour.

The umbrella kept the rain out of his face but his shoes and socks and trouser legs were already soaked. He hadn't even thought about where he was going. He wasn't ready to speak to Alison, not until he'd made up his mind what to say. For some reason he thought of Danny's father. Harry Grogan had spent a lifetime controlling others: his son, his wife, his shareholders, and a string of neglected mistresses. Grogan had controlled Nick once, buying his obedience for a hundred thousand dollars. What if Grogan was still controlling him?

A police car arrived and parked behind the ambulance. The police car's lights were flashing. The rain was coming down harder, bouncing off the tarmac like hail. His umbrella wasn't going to last long in this. He thought of turning back, of waiting inside the hospital until the storm was over.

Two of the spectators were holding a kind of tarpaulin sheet over the trolley in a vain effort to keep the patient dry. As the paramedics started wheeling the trolley towards the rear doors of the ambulance, Nick caught a glimpse of a green jacket, and some striped pyjamas.

The crowd was dispersing. The police, squatting in their fluorescent waterproofs, were examining some marks on the tarmac. Nick approached an off-duty nurse who had been among the crowd of bystanders. She looked shaken.

Nick couldn't help himself. 'Is he dead?'

The woman seemed as startled as he was by the directness of the question. She took a few moments to answer. 'I don't know.'

'What happened?'

'A car . . . they said it went straight for him.'

'Who? Who said?'

The woman shook her head. 'He was in his pyjamas.'

During all his years at the *Daily Star* Nick had never forgotten a story he'd written – especially if it made the front page. Walking away from the hospital carpark, he remembered the story of an Avis car mechanic, George Ruby, who used duplicate car rental agreements left in the glove box of returned vehicles to obtain false driver's licences. Ruby applied for welfare payments under each name. When he was finally arrested and charged, he had nearly a million dollars stashed in dozens of different bank accounts.

It wasn't greed that had brought George Ruby undone – hardly any of the stolen money had ever been spent – but the compulsion endlessly to repeat his crime: almost, Nick couldn't help thinking, as though his conscience obliged him to keep going until he was caught.

Nick had watched him in court, a sad, sinister-looking man, loyally attended every day by his sad, sinister-looking wife. He had noticed Ruby listening to the police prosecutor as if the crimes the prosecutor was describing had been committed by someone else altogether: a colleague, perhaps, or a neighbour whom Ruby knew casually but whose criminal tendencies came as a complete and devastating shock.

Nick thought about George Ruby and about that strange dissociation between the two versions of himself: Flash George the master forger and Hapless George the bewildered defendant. Until half an hour ago Nick had believed that he was in control of his life; now he realised he wasn't. But who was?

He picked up Homolka's taxi but left the 'For Hire' sign switched off. With the sign switched off, the taxi was a solitary place – and solitude was what Nick needed.

Was he stupid not to have seen Alison for what she was? But what was she – and what did she want from him? He thought of how she had looked at him on the morning they had brunch in Lygon Street – as if she knew something about him already. She had accused him of being inscrutable but she was the inscrutable one.

He thought about the way she addressed him when they were alone, never using his name – as if she couldn't bring herself to use the name 'Kevin', or couldn't bring herself to use it to him. If her brother was at the heart of this, then why had things come so far? He and Alison could have stopped at being friends. But they were more than friends. They may have deceived each other, they may have gone on deceiving each other, but not about that. She had lied to him, yes, but no more than he had lied to her – and would have continued lying to her. And what, after all, did Alison's lies amount to? How many lovers told each other the truth about themselves from the beginning? So their meeting wasn't the accident it seemed: did that really matter?

In two days Alison would be back and Nick would know the truth. The question was: how much did he want to know? He could live with deceit. He'd lived with it before. It was self-deceit that made life untenable.

He found himself, almost unconsciously, turning the corner into Drummond Street. He liked driving past her house, even when the lights were off and he knew she was thousands of kilometres away. The lights were off now. Nick pulled up and turned off his engine.

A group of white-shirted waiters was sitting over bowls of pasta in the Pizza-a-metro restaurant next door. One of the waiters recognised Nick and nodded. Nick nodded back. He wasn't sure why he was there. He got out and walked to the door.

The hall light was on. Nick pushed the bell and waited. Then he pushed it again. He waited a few seconds, then took the key out of his pocket and opened the door. The rain had soaked his back and shoulders.

It was clear that no one was home. Corby's bedroom door was slightly ajar. Nick opened it a few inches – far enough to catch a whiff of soiled clothes and stale marijuana smoke. Corby slept on a futon, which he never bothered to roll up. A blue plastic milk crate served as a bookcase for the library books Corby was always borrowing. After several terse conversations – Corby was always 'on his way out' as Nick walked through the door – it remained a mystery to Nick what he did for a living. Alison said he did some casual work at a boxing equipment shop in the Banana Alley Vaults near Flinders Street station. He left Corby's door as he'd found it and walked down the hallway.

From the bottom of the stairs Nick could see that Alison's bedroom door was open, which seemed strange. He walked into the kitchen and switched on the light. Corby's cereal bowl was sitting on the benchtop, with his tannin-stained Tweety-Pie coffee mug. There was an earthenware mug next to the kettle: one of a pair Alison had bought from a pottery shop in the Dandenongs during their first weekend together.

A glossy magazine was sitting on the sideboard. Nick didn't recognise the title – magazines opened and closed faster than humorously named Thai restaurants. He glanced at the cover-line: FIVE WAYS TO MAKE YOUR LOVER A NEW MAN. Almost every magazine Alison had ever bought contained a variation of the same story. The underlying message never changed: life would be so much happier, more comfortable, more fulfilling if you were a different person, if you were someone else. Nick himself had simply acted out the fantasy every glossy magazine dangled before its readers.

He checked the answering machine. The machine was on but the green light wasn't flashing. Nick pressed the 'Play' button. There were five messages, all from him. The most recent was more than a week old. Either nobody ever rang Corby or else he was always home to receive the call.

Slowly Nick climbed the stairs. He knew he shouldn't be here. At the same time he couldn't leave. The faint smell of Alison's perfume hung in the air. He could hear the steady drip-drip-drip of the shower head. The washers needed replacing and while Corby was strong enough to grind the taps shut, Alison wasn't. Suddenly Nick knew that she wasn't in Tokyo: she was here, in Melbourne.

Nick had never attempted to understand the complexities of the Qantas staffing roster. He knew Alison had to clock up a certain number of flight hours within a given roster period and that some routes were more sought-after than others for the hours they accumulated. And he knew that now and then she was placed on stand-by. During that time she might be called in at short notice or she might not. It sometimes occurred to Nick that for a flight attendant Alison didn't actually spend much time flying. He walked into her bedroom. He knew it was a violation – of her space, of her privacy – but he couldn't stop himself. Her uniform was hanging up and there, on top of the wardrobe, was her Qantas cabin bag.

She had lied about flying to Tokyo. Had she lied about other trips too? He'd dropped her at the airport in her Qantas uniform at least half a dozen times but she had always discouraged him from coming to meet her. Was that because she knew she wouldn't be there?

He went downstairs. How much did he really know about Alison – about the people she knew and the places she went? She had mentioned the names of various friends but Nick had never met a single one of them. There was Corby, of course. But Corby was different.

One of the kitchen drawers was stuffed with utility bills. Nick rummaged around until he came up with a telephone bill. He glanced at the calls to ISD numbers. Corby had called Alison once, for a minute and a half, at the Hotel Mulia Senayan in Jakarta two months ago, but that was all. Nick glanced down the page at the list of mobile calls. Several calls had been made to one number in particular. Nick stared at the last four digits: 7777. A sick feeling rose up from the pit of his stomach. He knew that number. It had been given to him by Danny Grogan's father.

A key was jiggling in the front door lock. Nick slammed the kitchen drawer shut.

'Hello,' said Alison, shutting the door behind her. She walked into the kitchen and kissed him warily on the lips. 'What are you doing here?'

'I thought you were in Tokyo,' said Nick.

'You didn't answer my question.'

They studied each other in silence.

'I came to fetch a shirt.'

Alison took off her coat. 'Which one?'

'Sorry?'

'Which shirt are you looking for?'

Nick said, 'You told me you were flying to Tokyo.'

'I was sick. I've been trying to ring you. Your phone's been off the hook.'

Nick didn't believe her. His phone had been off the hook, but he still didn't believe her. And he knew she didn't believe him. Standing there, Nick remembered a phrase from a French novel he'd once read: life was an unrelenting succession of lies. It had sounded trite at the time but now he realised how perceptive it was. Life was an unrelenting succession of lies. His own life. Alison's. Danny Grogan's. The only way to sustain those lies was by telling more lies – different lies, better lies. Every little slip required another lie to make things better. The process never stopped. It was like a mathematical sequence that went on and on, searching for an end point that didn't exist.

Nick said, 'Your cabin bag isn't packed.'

She laughed. 'Of course it isn't packed.'

'But you always pack your cabin bag the day before you fly.'

'What are you trying to say – that I'm not sick? For heaven's sake, I've got a doctor's note here to prove it.'

Nick knew he ought to go. After all he hadn't told Alison, he had no right to interrogate her. Maybe she was telling the truth about this. Maybe he'd just lost his ability to believe. 'I'm sorry,' he said. 'Coming here was a mistake.'

'Yes,' she replied. 'It was.'

*　　*　　*

Ian Stackpole was lying in a coma in the intensive care ward of the Royal Melbourne Hospital after what was described on page five of the *Herald-Sun* as a 'callous hit-and-run, just metres from the door of the casualty department'. An ironic undertone ran through the dozen or so paragraphs. Stackpole's brush with death in a hospital carpark appeared to have made the paper on oddity value alone and the reporter couldn't quite make up her mind whether the location made the victim lucky or unlucky.

Of course there was nothing in the report to suggest the accident could have been the result of mistaken identity: only one person knew that Stackpole had been wearing Nick's jacket when he was knocked down.

In fact some doubt remained as to whether Stackpole had been knocked down or whether he'd fallen and been struck where he lay. Either before or after he was hit, Stackpole had suffered a massive internal haemorrhage caused by a burst aorta. Nick wondered where (not to mention how) the reporter had got hold of this information, which would normally have been treated by the hospital as confidential. Now that he was comatose, Stackpole appeared to have surrendered his right to confidentiality.

None of these revelations altered the fact that he'd been hit by a car and that the driver had refused to stop – but it left some room for doubt, and doubt was what mattered to Nick now. As long as there was doubt, there was hope.

He drove into the city, parked the taxi and fed a handful of coins into the meter. The rain had stopped and shafts of watery sunlight penetrated the clouds. The pavements were beginning to steam. Strangers bumped into him, as though oblivious to his physical presence. He felt like a walking ghost, a mass of confused thoughts and quivering nerves. A derelict was sitting on a strip of cardboard outside a pawnbroker's shop with a biscuit tin between his legs. A handwritten sign around his neck said: 'No home. No work. No money.'

Apart from a few coins and a packet of cigarettes, the biscuit tin was empty. Nick stopped and took a twenty-dollar note out of his wallet and placed it in the tin. The vacant expression on the derelict's face didn't change. He stared through Nick as though he didn't exist. Maybe he was right, Nick thought. *Maybe I don't exist.*

That night, a man named Kevin Michael Chambers burnt to death in a rented house in West Sunshine. According to the *Age*, the dead man had been living at that address for less than a week. The fire appeared to have started in the living room, probably while Chambers was asleep. He had probably been asphyxiated by fumes from the nylon carpets long before the flames reached him.

Although officially unemployed and on the dole, Chambers had been doing very well out of the illegal economy: working for cash as a labourer on building sites and driving a cab at night, also for cash and without a licence. He was thirty-three years old. There was a small photograph of the victim, taken on the pier at St Kilda with a diminutive black woman identified as his mother, Grace. Apart from the afro hair, there was nothing about the pale-skinned man that identified him as the black woman's son.

Nick had been driving all night. He'd filled the tank twice. According to the odometer, he'd travelled more than four hundred kilometres – and yet Nick had no recollection of where he'd been. Strangely, he wasn't tired. At some point he must have pulled over and slept for a while. There was a packet of Winfields on the passenger seat beside him, and some butts in the ashtray. He wondered how they had got there. He lit another cigarette. How long was it since he'd spoken to Alison? It felt like days, not hours. The memory of it seemed to belong to a dream, a bad dream, the sort that returned long after you had woken up.

He was parked outside a Pizza Hut restaurant in Footscray. It was raining again. The early-morning traffic splashed down Ballarat Road. Nick looked at his watch. The time was 6.42 a.m.

First a man incinerated in his vehicle by a bolt of lightning in south-west Sydney. Then a patient knocked down in a hospital carpark wearing a borrowed jacket. Now a man asphyxiated in a house fire in West Sunshine. Nick felt responsible for all three.

He rested his head against the steering wheel. He'd stood up in court and told a harmless lie, and somehow it had led to this. He didn't understand how or why. All he knew was that he was not in control of his life and hadn't been since the day he said yes to Harry Grogan. Perhaps, now and then, he'd done something to alter its course in one way or another: he'd made one choice rather than another, gone ahead when he should have paused, said 'yes' when the prudent answer would have been 'no' or 'maybe'. But in the greater scheme of things none of that mattered. Fate, or luck, or something had delivered him here, to this exact point, and there was no way back.

His mobile phone was ringing. He could see from the caller

ID that it was Alison. Her voice sounded different, but different to what? The last twenty-four hours had changed everything. They had changed Alison. And they had changed him.

'It's me,' she said. 'Where are you?'

He told her.

'Have you read the paper?'

He knew at once that she was talking about the fire.

'What's happening?'

'I don't know.'

'I'm scared,' she said. 'I'm scared for both of us.'

As he turned the key in the ignition Nick glanced at himself in the mirror. He had a cigarette between his fingers. A fine stubble of hair was growing back. For the first time in many months he studied his reflection and saw not Kevin Chambers but Nick Carmody.

He was going to need Grogan's money. Whatever happened, he was going to need Grogan's money. He couldn't predict what Alison was going to tell him, or what she would insist on being told, but he knew things couldn't go on as they were. Alison had known from the beginning that he wasn't the person he was pretending to be, and yet she'd let him act out his charade – almost, he thought, as if she was calling his bluff, daring him to make a mistake.

He drove home and parked outside his house. The fly screen was open and the front door slightly ajar. Nick sat there for a while, watching for movement behind the venetian blinds. He picked up his mobile phone to call the police. What was he waiting for? He could pretend to be a passer-by, a neighbour walking his dog. His mind raced ahead. He couldn't wait for the police. By now it was clear, in any case, that there was nobody inside the house.

Walking up the garden path, he could see that the door wasn't ajar: it had been wrenched off its hinges. Something else was wrong. The dog wasn't barking. She slept in a kennel in the yard but she knew the sound of Nick's footsteps.

He walked along the side path, between the house and the rotten timber fence. A galvanised iron gate separated the rectangle of scorched earth at the front from the dead grass and cracked concrete at the rear. A rusty padlock hung from the bolt, giving the impression that the gate was locked, although the padlock didn't work.

The gate hadn't been opened. The broken padlock was exactly as he'd left it. He stood there and whistled twice. The dog didn't come. Nick unhooked the padlock, opened the gate and walked slowly around to the back of the house.

The remains of a raw chicken carcass lay on the hot cement, encased within a moving crust of black flies. The greyhound had never been able to resist the offer of food. Kicking the carcass over, Nick noticed white powder sticking to the skin: some kind of poison. The gizzards were lying in a plastic bag nearby.

A thin grey paw protruded from the kennel. The dog's chin was lathered with foam but its skin was already cold. Nick felt the tears welling in his eyes. He knelt down and gently stroked its velvet skull. He hadn't expected this. Whatever it was he'd expected, it wasn't this. This was the dog's reward for all the helpless love it had shown him. Nick took the ragged tartan blanket out of the kennel and draped it over the lifeless animal. He wished he had time to do more.

The house had been turned over from front to back. There wasn't a cupboard that hadn't been trashed, a drawer that hadn't been pulled out and emptied. The burglar had found the bundle of company cheques made out to cash that Nick had hidden beneath the bottom drawer of his chest of drawers. His digital camera was gone, and a couple of dozen CDs. Nick saw the remains of a joint ground into the living-room carpet. The burglary had been thorough but not professional: the burglar had been distracted before he could finish. He hadn't found, or hadn't looked for, the key to the garage, and the garage was where Nick had hidden Kevin Chambers' passport. It took him several minutes to find it, stashed behind a small mountain of paint tins. Until now, he'd never thought of using it. The possibility of passing himself off as the person in the photograph was just too remote. But Nick had few options left. He held the photograph up to the light. There was a certain facial resemblance, but Kevin Chambers' hair was down to his shoulders and it was peroxide blond. Maybe that was to Nick's advantage. The passport was more than seven years old.

Nick flicked through it. Apart from a few days in Bali in 1999, Chambers hadn't been out of Australia, not on this pass- port, anyway.

Before leaving, Nick did his best to hang the front door back on its hinges – to make it appear, at least from the street, as if nothing was wrong. It wouldn't be long, he realised, before the dog started to smell and one of the neighbours called the police, but by then he and Alison would be far away.

* * *

Alison came to the door in her pyjamas. Nick didn't attempt to kiss her and she didn't offer her face to be kissed. She flattened herself against the wall to allow him to pass. Then she shut the door behind him.

The light in the hall had blown. Nick walked through the darkness to the kitchen. There was a bitter, metallic taste in his mouth. He needed a shower.

Alison followed him and stood in the doorway, as if she couldn't allow herself to come any closer.

'Aren't you going to say something?'

'What do you want me to say?'

'You could start by telling me who you are. I mean, who you really are.'

'You know who I am.'

'I know who you're pretending to be. You're pretending to be a man called Kevin Michael Chambers.'

For a long while Nick didn't say anything. It crossed his mind, at least for a few seconds, to try to bluff it out. But it was too late for that. And Alison deserved more. He could argue that he wasn't pretending to be anyone, that all he'd wanted from the beginning was to escape from the problems of being Nick Carmody by taking someone else's name. His intention had never been to impersonate Kevin Chambers, just to duplicate him. But it was all semantics – and Alison probably wouldn't believe him anyway.

'I needed a name,' said Nick. 'I found one in the glove box of a car. I didn't know anything about the person it belonged to. I didn't want to know anything. I was afraid of who I was and I thought I'd be safer for a while being someone else.'

Alison studied him in silence, not just his face but his hands, his arms, as if the truth or falseness of the words he'd just spoken was etched on his skin. 'Kevin Chambers is my brother,' she said. 'But I'm sure you've worked that out by now.'

It felt as though they were staring at each other through miles of space. The kitchen table was like a continent between them. The newspaper was lying there, open at the report of the fire in West Sunshine.

'He sells drugs,' she said. 'And he informs on other people who sell drugs. He's not a good person, my brother.'

Drug dealer. Police informant. It was clear to Nick why Chambers had enemies, and why those enemies were trying to kill him. 'How long is it since you've seen him?' he asked.

'Four years,' said Alison. 'Maybe five. We've never been close. I was only ever a source of money.'

'You bought him a car,' said Nick.

'Yes, I bought him a car.' Her voice was full of hurt and disappointment. 'I paid for it and got it registered. He told me he needed one. He said he was driving to the west. I didn't ask where. I didn't want to know. I got a letter from an insurance company saying the car had been involved in an accident in Melbourne. I knew it couldn't be him. My brother was known in Melbourne. And the people who knew him didn't like him. I realised a stranger was driving my brother's car – someone who didn't know much about him. So I hired someone, a private investigator, to find out who.'

Nick remembered the dark-haired man in the fawn suit, the one he'd caught sight of from time to time during his first few weeks driving Homolka's taxi.

'It didn't take him long to find you. Don't ask me how. He showed me a photograph. He even caught you on video. And

211

guess what – you hadn't just taken his car, you'd taken his name as well. The likeness was very convincing. I could see straight away how people were fooled. But I'm his sister. You didn't walk like Kevin. It was the walk that gave it away. I paid him his money and then I came here myself. I wanted to know what kind of man would want to impersonate my brother.'

'The accident,' said Nick. 'You planned it.'

'I'd watched you take that route before. Every Friday in fact. I thought if I waited for you I could make it look like an accident. I made a bit of a mess of it.'

Nick stood up and walked to the window. 'Why didn't you say anything?'

'I wanted to give you the chance to tell me yourself.' She laughed bitterly. 'Until last night I actually believed you would.'

She was convincing, and Nick wanted desperately to be convinced: that they had really loved each other, that he hadn't imagined it all.

'What did Grogan offer you?'

'Who?'

'Harry Grogan. Did he promise not to harm me? Did he say it was for my own safety? He must have told you something. Did Grogan tell you I lied to keep his son out of jail?'

'Jail? What are you talking about? I've never met Harry Grogan. What's he got to do with any of this?'

'I've seen your telephone bill. You called Harry Grogan three times.'

'I'm not the only one who lives here.'

Slowly the truth dawned on him. Danny's father had tracked him down and now he was having him watched, but it wasn't Alison doing the watching. It was Corby. Corby the loner, with his odd ways and his nocturnal habits. Corby the opportunist, with his part-time job and his mortgage. It was Corby, he realised, who'd made the hoax taxi booking for Nick Carmody. Corby was Harry Grogan's spy. And if Corby had been spying on him, he'd been spying on Alison too. But what if Corby was more than that? What if Grogan was behind the killings? Grogan might want Nick out of the way, but not without knowing what had happened to the cheques. It was Corby who'd ransacked the house and found the cheques. Nick suddenly felt hot, as though he was going to faint.

'We have to go,' he said.

'Not until you tell me everything,' said Alison. Her fists were clenched. She seemed rooted to the floor, like a statue.

'I'll tell you everything. Trust me. But not now. There isn't time.'

Trust me. How often had he said those words before: to informants, to readers, to ordinary credulous members of the Australian public? Trust me not to reveal who supplied this information. Trust me to get the facts right. Trust me with the precious photograph of your dead son and I'll make sure you get it back. *Trust me.* Even to his own ears, the plea felt absurd.

Alison was shaking her head. She looked scared. 'Go away where?'

'Anywhere. Without telling Corby. Without telling anyone.'

For a few moments she didn't speak. She seemed to be holding her breath, as if by holding it long enough she could enter some new state in which all of this could be forgotten. 'But what about your dog? You can't just leave a dog to look after itself.'

'I'll get someone to feed the dog. We can drive straight to the airport. We'll book somewhere by phone.'

Alison was looking at him as though he was mad. Perhaps he was mad. Perhaps they both were.

She came down the stairs, dragging a Samsonite suitcase.

'We'll take your car,' he said. 'We'll leave it in the long-stay carpark.'

Alison didn't answer.

'We'll tell the agent it's an impromptu holiday,' he said, throwing her suitcase into the back seat. 'We'll take the first place they suggest.'

There was a travel agency just around the corner in Lygon Street. Alison dialled the number as they drove past. After a few minutes she said, 'There's a flight to Tahiti that leaves just after lunch. We can pay by credit card and collect our tickets at the airport.'

Nick hesitated. Cash was harder to follow. But it was too late to worry about that now.

'Why not,' he said.

The check-in clerk at Tullamarine Airport scarcely looked at Nick's passport before handing him his ticket and boarding pass.

While Alison went in search of bottled water Nick stood at an observation window and watched planes taking off and landing. He felt different, changed in some elemental way from the person he had been when he entered Alison's house. She returned with two bottles of water and handed him one. He wondered whether she had telephoned Corby. He no longer knew what she was capable of – or what he was capable of, for that matter.

The departure lounge was full and then the plane was too

crowded and the engines too noisy for them to talk, and yet talking was the only thing that was going to save them. Night came quickly once they were airborne. Alison was asleep or pretending to be. Among three hundred people, packed together like sardines, he felt shockingly alone. Somehow the hours passed. Pinpricks of light twinkled far below – the lights of tiny Pacific islands and of boats adrift in the immensity of the ocean. Otherwise there was nothing but black sea and black sky and the dancing image of an in-flight movie he was too preoccupied to listen to.

The plane landed at Papeete just after 11 p.m. local time. Nick reached for Alison's hand. She didn't pull it away but nor did she return his squeeze. The humidity as they walked across the tarmac was suffocating. Nick imagined security guards waiting for him inside the terminal – jumpy men with guns and walkie-talkies.

A welcoming phalanx of Tahitian women in traditional costumes greeted visitors with garlands of fragrant white flowers. Nick lowered his head to receive one. Looking around, Alison smiled – her first smile since they'd left Australia. 'It suits you,' she said.

There were armed police everywhere. A young man in a brown uniform and shoulder holster was waving them towards the immigration counter. Nick walked forwards and pushed his passport through the glass. He smiled stiffly at the female official, who didn't smile back. She glanced at the photograph before flicking through the pages of his passport. She typed something into her computer. The man in the brown uniform wandered over, murmured a few words in her ear, and walked away. The official picked up Alison's passport.

Any second now Nick expected to see police closing in. He suddenly felt ridiculous. He pictured himself on the front page of the *Daily Star*, handcuffed, wearing a garland of white flowers.

The immigration official was handing back Alison's passport. She gazed from one to the other and said. 'You can go, Monsieur. Madame.'

On the other side of the immigration desk groups of smiling women held up placards bearing the names of big hotels. A beautiful Tahitian woman and an equally good-looking young man in traditional dress were holding a sign that said DREAM-LAND. Behind it stood a whiteboard bearing a list of names: Shaw, Truman, Mercer (x2), Theobald, Lal (x2), Sarkozy, Ostell.

Not long ago the Australian papers had been full of slavish praise for the new Dreamland Pacific resort, with its palm-thatched bungalows and its swim-up casino and its imported chefs. Dreamland Pacific was the jewel in Harry Grogan's crown, the last word in opulence – a monument to hubris and fraudulent accounting that in a few short years would be flattened by a tropical typhoon. That was Dreamland: a vision and an illusion, uninsured and uninsurable.

'We'll need some local money,' said Nick. 'I've only got a few dollars.' The bureau de change was closed for the night, but outside the terminal building Nick could see a branch of the Banque de Polynésie, complete with automatic teller machine.

Nick noticed that the man in the brown uniform had followed them through immigration. He seemed to be waiting for Nick to do something.

'I'm going to find the bathroom,' said Alison. 'Will you look after my suitcase?'

Nick fed his credit card into the teller machine and typed some numbers and waited for the cash to appear. People were gathering around the DREAMLAND sign.

It was an under-thirty-fives group – the sort of group that he and Alison could get lost in. Names were crossed off the whiteboard and the new arrivals were herded towards an air-conditioned minivan standing outside the airport terminal.

Nick counted his money. Alison had been gone nearly ten minutes. He wondered what was keeping her. Had she changed her mind? He was asking her to wait, to be patient, but what had he done to deserve her patience? If their situations had been reversed, would he have waited?

All the names on the whiteboard had been crossed out except one: Truman. The beautiful couple representing Dreamland were looking at their watches and conferring. It was past midnight and the resort's other guests were all aboard the minibus; Nick had watched a porter loading their luggage onto a steel trailer. There was still no sign of Alison. Perhaps she was lost. He looked over his shoulder at the waiting minibus. Impatient faces were pressed against the windows. Other passengers were already asleep.

There were so many doors. The walls of the terminal building seemed to consist of nothing but doors. Was Alison behind one of them: an unwilling betrayer? One of the doors opened and closed again. Or a willing betrayer? Had he expected too much of her? He should not have left her alone. They should have stayed together.

Nick stood with their two bags at his feet. This wasn't working out as it was supposed to. He'd begged Alison to trust him and yet he couldn't bring himself to trust her. If he owed her anything, he owed her the whole truth, but the whole truth was too much. It would leave him with nothing. How much truth could he give? How much truth could she bear?

The low tropical clouds had burst and rain was slanting in under the awning. He loved Alison – more, perhaps, than he'd loved anyone – but love was no longer enough. He looked at his watch. Soon he would see her walking towards him.

There was still no sign of Truman. The good-looking young man was folding up the whiteboard while his colleague gently ushered a fractious passenger back on board the bus. Suddenly Nick knew what he was going to do. If he didn't act now, it would be too late. He didn't expect Alison to forgive him at once but in the end she would realise it was the only way: he was doing this for both of them.

The beautiful Tahitian tour guide was returning his smile. The sickening sadness he had felt on the plane lifted, like a weight that had been physically taken from him. His body seemed to quiver with nervous energy. He felt a surge of confidence, as if he'd done this before. Because he had done this before. He'd been doing it all his life, pretending to be somebody else. And he had a talent for it. Being somebody else was the only way he knew how to be himself. He put Alison's suitcase behind a pillar.

'Monsieur Truman,' said the tour guide, reaching for his bag. 'We were starting to wonder where you were.'